UNCONDITIONALLY MINE

NADINE GONZALEZ

MILLS & BOON

First Published in Great Britain 2018
by Mills & Boon, an imprint of HarperCollins*Publishers*
1 London Bridge Street, London, SE1 9GF

Unconditionally Mine © 2018 Nadine Seide

ISBN: 978-0-263-26523-1

0818

MIX
Paper from
responsible sources
FSC™ C007454

This book is produced from independently certified FSC™ paper to ensure responsible forest management.

For more information visit: www.harpercollins.co.uk/green

Printed and bound in Spain
by CPI, Barcelona

For Ariel, my love, and Nathaniel, my heart.

For Stephanie, Katherine, Melissa, Ericka, Alexander and Andrew. The future is yours.

Acknowledgments

I am grateful to the editors at Kimani Press: Shannon Criss, Glenda Howard and Keyla Hernandez. Special thanks to Keyla for being the best first editor an author could have. Your patience and dedication to authentic storytelling is greatly appreciated. I wish you all the best in the future.

Chapter 1

Sofia cupped the bottle of Dom Pérignon and released the cork. *Pop!* She poured the overflow into a glass and took a sip. Like water into sand. *When was the last time I'd opened a bottle and had some non-work-related fun,* she wondered. Short answer: her engagement party. But that didn't count. The formal event had been organized at her mother's request. And since that night, over a year ago, life had gone stale. No joy, no fizz, no pop.

This, however, was no time for a pity party. Sofia had an actual party—cocktails and hors d'oeuvres for fifty—to wrap up. Real life was work. Whoever promised her fizz and pop, anyway?

Sofia rested her champagne glass on the counter—a treat for later—took a deep breath and handed out her orders. "Melissa, please set up the champagne flutes... Ericka, where's the box with the trays?"

The kitchen door creaked open. Expecting one of the waiters, she frowned at the guest peering in. Ground zero—in this case, a French country kitchen in the host's Coral Gables home—was a madhouse. Guests weren't welcome. And this guest... *Jesus!* He was two hundred pounds of muscle beautifully packaged in a heather-gray suit. She took in his toasty brown skin and intelligent brown eyes, and cleared her throat. "May I help you?"

"Some water...please."

"Melissa, get this gentleman a glass of water."

"A bottle, if you have it."

Melissa held open the refrigerator door. "Would you prefer sparkling or flat?"

"Flat."

"Spring or—"

"Melissa, please!" Sofia cried. The man shouldn't have to answer a quiz.

Melissa handed him a small FIJI bottle. "Here you go." She smiled shyly.

He smiled too, but there was nothing shy about it. Sofia stiffened. She felt the oddest sensation, the turn of a dial.

But with Watergate resolved and the guest gone, she focused on the task at hand. "Guys, the toast is in five minutes. Let's go!"

Melissa lined up a row of champagne flutes, giggling as she worked. "That guy was so hot I nearly fell on my face."

Ericka piled a dozen silver trays on the counter. "I thought you were only into pretty boys."

"Comes a time in every woman's life to forget the boys and find a man," Melissa said.

"You're a woman now?" Ericka asked.

Valid question. Melissa was only nineteen and looked even younger. But now was not the time to delve into it.

"Quiet!" Sofia snapped. "I need to focus."

Everybody fell silent. She took a breath and started pouring from the bottle of Dom. The host, a hotshot Miami lawyer, was throwing this party for his firm. This wasn't the usual office party fare. Normally, they'd serve coconut shrimp and California sparkling wine. This event was all about grilled scallops, crab cakes, smoked salmon topped with caviar, top-shelf liquor and fine champagne. For that reason, she'd taken on the task of filling the glasses herself—not that she was any good at it. It required steady hands, and she was anything but calm.

"Can I help?"

Damn! The words were spoken so close to her ear, she jumped and nearly spilled two hundred dollars' worth of champagne down her shirt. Him again! What was he doing back in the kitchen? She straightened up to better confront him. His eyes had flecks of gold. One sip of champagne would do that to you; make you see all the sparkle in the world.

She clutched the bottle to her chest. "You really shouldn't be here."

He slipped off his suit jacket, revealing a gorgeous garnet lining, and draped it over a chair. Sofia's mother owned a fabric shop and Sofia had her eye for quality.

"Don't worry," he said. "I used to be a waiter."

So what? Hadn't everyone?

Over her protests, he confiscated the bottle of champagne. Then she watched as he expertly poured eight glasses with a sure hand, not spilling one precious drop. Those brown hands…the nails were clean and clipped, but there was no mistaking them for the hands of a gentleman. If he applied even the slightest pressure, the thick green bottle might shatter.

"How many glasses do you need me to fill?" he asked.

"I don't *need* you to do anything," Sofia replied. "I'd love for you to join the party and enjoy your evening."

She couldn't drop the show of indignation. She had employees to impress. He glanced up at her. Brown eyes like rum swirling into a glass.

"Fifty," she said. "Plus an extra ten. You never know."

"Well, line 'em up."

Melissa handed him bottle after bottle. Ericka loaded up the trays. Sofia stood to the side, watching her team and this stranger work quietly and efficiently together. The door swung open again. A young guy, a lawyer-in-the-making type, poked his head in. "What are you doing in here? Everyone's looking for you."

"Okay," he said. "I'm done!"

Sofia inspected his work. All sixty champagne flutes were filled to equal height, ready to go. He reached for his jacket. On his way out, he turned to her and said pointedly, "You're welcome."

She shrugged. He wasn't worth sparring with—because for sure she'd lose. Her staff, though, cheered the unlikely hero.

"Give me a break!" Sofia groaned. "He poured champagne!"

"But he did it with style!" Melissa declared.

"Let's stay on schedule," Sofia said. "Ericka, have the waiters serve the host and the guest of honor first."

Her troops went out and returned with news. "You won't believe it! Mr. I-Used-To-Be-A-Waiter? *He*'s the guest of honor. He's out there giving a speech. This party is for *him*."

Sofia popped a crab cake in her mouth. *Interesting*. He must have been nervous and slumming in the kitchen was his way to take the edge off.

"That's so cool, don't you think?" Melissa said.

There was no time to think. The kitchen door swung open again and this time a woman burst in. She was stunning with a caramel complexion and cheekbones that ought to be insured, but her features were distorted. Tears streaming down her cheeks made tar of her mascara. "I need a drink! Give me something, anything."

Sofia braced herself. What roller-coaster ride was this?

Melissa offered her a bottle of water. The woman huffed. "Do I look like I need water?"

Sofia sent her employees away and took over. She grabbed a bottle of Patrón and a couple of glasses and guided the woman to a table by the kitchen's fantastic bay windows. She poured generously and began her usual speech to calm unruly party guests. "I don't know you or what you're going through—"

"I'll tell you."

Oh, boy.

"He was only supposed to be with us a few weeks!" Her Brazilian accent produced petal-soft *o*'s and *u*'s. "I thought, why not have a little fun?"

Sofia knew instinctively who *he* was. She spotted him through the window out by the pool, sipping from a glass of champagne that he'd poured. He looked radiant in the fading September sun. His dark hair was cut short, barely visible, and it didn't matter because his thick brows framed his face beautifully. But that was neither here nor there.

"I should've known they were going to recruit him. They all love him at the firm. He has a nickname and everything."

"What's the nickname?"

"What?" the woman asked.

Sofia flushed. "Never mind."

"The Gun."

Sofia poured some tequila for herself and wondered how he might've earned it. It couldn't have been looks alone.

The woman read her mind. "He's that good."

Okay, then.

"They asked him to stay and he said yes. Things were great between us. We had this amazing connection, so I figured—"

"You figured wrong." Sofia didn't need GPS to figure out where this story was heading.

The woman slammed her glass on the marble-top table. Tequila flew everywhere.

Sofia reached for a napkin and wiped up the mess. The hostess was really fond of her antique furniture.

"I've seen him." Sofia pointed out the window, but "The Gun" was no longer out there. "The man is a shot of rum and he went straight to your head. But you can't afford to fall apart like this. You work with these people, and you'll have to face them all on Monday. Mess up and I promise you the catty bitches out there won't ever let you live it down. And I'm not talking about the women."

Sofia assumed the silence that followed her little speech was a well-earned response. Then it stretched out a beat too long and something in the way the woman gripped her glass warned her that they were no longer alone.

How much had he heard?

The woman rose from the table, brushed tequila droplets off her dress and strode out of the kitchen without uttering a word.

Sofia sat with her back to the door and didn't move until she heard it creak shut and she was certain he was gone. When you thought about it, she'd done *him* a favor—a big one. Life had a way of leveling the score.

So, Mr. Gun...you're welcome.

Chapter 2

Five months later...

Jon had expected nothing until she walked in. Then, suddenly, his morning burst open with possibilities. After a glance around the auditorium, she picked a seat near him. Was it coincidence or the might of his will? He watched her drop her massive purse on one of the three empty seats between them, effectively erecting a wall. She crossed her golden-brown legs and went about the careful business of removing her sunglasses. Her profile was partially obstructed by a cloud of reddish-brownish curls flowing past her shoulders, but he made out the fringe of her lashes, the upward curve of her nose and a carefully drawn mouth.

It was going to be a lovely day.

"Please rise for Judge Antoine Roland."

Jon rose. He couldn't shake creeping déjà vu. Had they met before and where?

Judge Roland welcomed the drowsy assembly to the Miami-Dade County jury pool. After a reminder of the importance of jury duty in the great scheme of American democracy, he led the assembly in reciting the Pledge of Allegiance. When he was done, some applauded—but not too many. The judge exited the auditorium as solemnly as he had entered. With that over, the oddly familiar woman sat and mumbled, "Let's get this over with."

He took it as an opening. "*That's* the spirit."

She looked his way, as if seeing him for the first time. Another announcement stopped him from introducing himself.

"Please fill out the jury questionnaire as best you can," a clerk said through the piercing feedback of a microphone. "Don't lose it. You'll have to hand it to the bailiff when you're called. And, if you're eligible, don't forget to request a reimbursement form. It's only fifteen dollars, but times are hard. In the meantime, enjoy the movie. Julia Roberts—she's always fun. The snack bar is open. Plus, there's the quiet room if you prefer to read. All in all, it's going to be a long day, folks! So why not make a friend?"

She immediately shot to her feet. Jon figured he'd scared her away, but she only went as far as the front desk to request the forms. Then for five minutes or so, she sat quietly, brows drawn, filling in each document using a pen retrieved from the depths of her bottomless purse. It was a fountain pen with some weight to it. The ink was a brilliant indigo blue. When she was done, she carefully replaced the pen's cap, and he noticed her fingers, long and slim with deep red lacquered nails.

She turned in one form, kept the other, returned to her seat and folded those beautiful hands on her lap. Without looking at him, she said, "You're nosy."

"Observant," he said. "And so are you, but you're better at it."

She swiveled in her seat and studied him, her wide brown eyes taking him apart and stitching him back together. He waited, counting the seconds for her to draw her conclusions. Women either loved him or hated him. There was never any middle ground. If she fell into the wrong camp, he had ways to drag her across the line.

Her eyes narrowed. "Have we…?"

"Slept together?" he asked. "I don't think so. I would've remembered."

If he was hoping to rattle her, it didn't work.

"I remember you," she said drily.

There was little evidence that the memory was a pleasant one.

"I knew we'd met before," he said. "Now clue me in. It's been driving me crazy."

She reached into her purse for earbuds and plugged them into her phone. "Sorry. Not trying to be rude, but all I want is to get through jury duty in peace."

"You heard the clerk. Let's be friends. My name is Jon—in case you'd forgotten."

"I have enough friends."

"Your friends are not like me." He got up and buttoned his suit jacket. "I'll get us coffee. Then you can tell me the story of us."

She surprised him by rising to her feet. Even on impressively high heels—the sexiest pumps he'd seen in a while—she only reached his chin. "I can get my own coffee."

"Let's each get our own coffee together," he proposed. "My treat."

She grunted and took the lead. He happily followed, feeling like a winner. In a room full of dull and disgruntled people, she had brought light and something else that he needed: a challenge. Ten minutes in, he didn't know her name or their shared history. He was going to have to work for it.

The snack bar offered Cuban coffee, Cuban toast, Cuban breakfast pastries and a Cuban breakfast special priced at $3.99. While they waited in line, he asked her what she'd like.

"Coffee with lots of milk. But don't worry. I'll order."

"I'm not worried."

The woman at the register took one look at him and made a suggestion. "American coffee?"

"No," he said. *"Un cortadito y un café con leche bien claro."*

He paid and stuffed a five-dollar bill in the tip jar. She watched him with an amused smile.

"What's the matter?" he asked.

"Do you really speak Spanish? Or just know how to order coffee?"

He wanted to stay on topic. "You were about to tell me how we met."

"No, I wasn't," she said. "If you can't remember, it's best to leave it in the past."

"Who said that? Aristotle?"

The cashier tapped on the glass partition to get his attention. Their order was ready. Jon grabbed both cups and held hers up and out of reach. "Here you go…" He gave her a chance to fill in the blank.

She folded her arms across her chest, her generous chest. "My name is Sofia."

The name didn't ring any bells.

"Nice to meet you again, Sofia." He handed over her coffee. "Should we check out the quiet room?"

"Too much quiet and I'll start crying," she said wearily. "Let's just find a place to sit."

Slot machines in Vegas weren't as loud as those going off in his mind.

She led him to the far end of the auditorium to an empty row of chairs under a window. Sunlight exposed the dust in the air, like so many microscopic angels. They sat closer this time, shoulders touching, and he wondered what she'd have to cry about. Instead, he asked why she'd filled out a wage reimbursement form.

She shot him a look. Her brown eyes sparkled in the sunlight. She was very lovely.

"You *are* observant," she said.

"We've established that." It was no mystery. She'd filled out two forms and he'd filled only one.

"My time is worth money. That's why. Not that it's your business."

"We're talking fifteen dollars for an eight-hour day, right? You've got to be worth more than that."

He was aware that he sounded like an elitist ass. Fifteen dollars was plenty for anyone who needed it. As the clerk had said, times were hard. But her sunglasses were Tom Ford, and that enormous purse was Louis Vuitton.

"I'm self-employed," she said. "And to be honest, I've got a couple of toll violations. The state of Florida might as well pay for them."

He laughed. She was a hustler. He could fall in love with this girl.

"You know what?" she snapped. "I hope you get stuck in jury duty all week."

"Not going to happen. They won't pick me."

"Why not?" She took a sip of coffee. "Are you a felon? If you tell them, they'll let you go home. It's unfortunate, but it's the law."

Jon carefully lifted the lid of his mini Styrofoam cup and blew on the frothy surface. "Do I look like a felon?"

"Honestly?"

Jon had no illusions. His bulk intimidated some. His weathered face didn't hide that he'd been punched more than a few times. An ex once told him that his expensive clothes only sharpened his rough edges. He gestured to the form lying flat on her lap. "Show me yours and I'll show you mine."

A typical jury questionnaire had more information than

any online dating profile, and Jon liked to have all the facts up front.

She brought her cup to her lips to hide a smile. "I haven't fallen for that since ever."

"You can trust me," he said.

"Before coffee I don't trust my own mother," she said.

He reached into his breast pocket and pulled out his form, folded in squares. She hesitated, then snatched it from his hands. He took note of the things she chose to read.

"Jonathan Gunther. Thirty-two. Single. No kids. Attorney, criminal defense…"

She stopped reading and glanced up at him.

"They never pick lawyers," he said with a wink. "We can turn a shoplifting case into a constitutional crisis."

"Criminal *defense*?"

"Is that going to be a problem?" he asked. "I won't bring my clients home."

"You're the problem," she said with a smile.

That smile could light up the world, Jon thought. "Your turn."

She handed over her form, but he didn't take it. "Why don't you tell me what's there?"

She pressed her lips together. "Let's see… Sofia Silva. Twenty-nine. Event planner."

"A party girl?" he asked.

"I'm an entrepreneur, an award-winning small business owner." She frowned. "You have a strange way of making friends."

"I thought you had enough friends. I put us on another track."

"Don't. You're wasting your time."

"Why?" he asked. "Married? Kids?"

She read from the questionnaire as if she'd forgotten

what she'd written. He knew it was all to avoid making eye contact. "No kids—yet. One significant other."

Jon took another sip of coffee. Normally, this would be his cue to back off. But she'd stirred things up, and there was no quick way to calm those things down.

The clerk assembled a panel, calling out numbers like lottery picks. One by one, those selected gathered their things and stumbled out of the room. The room fell silent again with Julia Roberts's laughter for pleasant background noise.

"Why defend criminals?" she asked.

"Criminals are just people who've made bad choices."

"Or they're selfish and stupid people with complete disregard for others."

"*Callous* disregard," Jon said. "Sounds better."

She moaned. "You really are a lawyer."

"One of the best." He handed her a business card. "Next time a client tries to sue you, you'll be glad you know me."

She laughed at the joke and took the card. Another panel was assembled and time passed. It was easy talking with her. She was sharp; nothing he said went untested. But a pattern was emerging. She'd fire questions at him but carefully avoided revealing anything about herself.

"You've tried cases at this courthouse?" she asked.

"No. Federal court."

"Are your clients killers?"

"*Alleged* killers, you mean," he said. "And no, they're not. They're alleged Ponzi schemers, tax evaders and embezzlers."

"Can you name some of your clients?"

"Don't think I don't know what you're doing."

"What's that?"

"The one-sided conversation. I invented that trick."

"All I've done is ask a few questions," she said defensively. "If you weren't so careful, you wouldn't mind."

"Careful? No one's ever accused me of that."

"Not an accusation," she said. "An observation. You're careful with words."

"I'm good with words."

"You're not at all modest," she observed.

"Not even a little," he said. "I'll note that we have a past that you're trying to bury. So who's being careful here?"

She held him in her soft brown gaze. "But if you can't remember our past, does it exist?"

"And if a tree fell in the forest...?"

The clerk returned to the microphone, this time to announce an extended lunch break. He invited her out to eat.

"I'm going to pick up a salad at the medical campus across the street," she said. "You're welcome to come with."

They rode the elevator to the courthouse ground floor. Outside, the aroma rising from the hot-dog carts made him nostalgic for New York City. With a hand on her elbow, he steered her across the street toward the parking lot. His Porsche was parked in an open lot reserved for jurors. Its steel-blue glaze matched the hazy Florida sky.

She yanked her arm free. "We can walk to the salad place. It's not far."

"We're not going to the salad place. I heard there are seafood restaurants along the river not far from here."

She came to a full stop in the middle of the street. "I'm not getting in your car."

She really didn't trust him. He wondered what he'd done to her? And why couldn't he remember? He was sharper than this.

"I'll bring you back in one piece," he promised from the sidewalk. "How else will you collect your fifteen bucks?"

She stood rooted in place, stubborn. A patrol car turned

a corner and signaled a warning for her to move out of the way. This was her chance to escape; all she'd have to do was turn and run. They locked eyes, engaging in a mental arm-wrestling match. Another whirl of the police siren propelled her into motion. Picking up the pace, she made her way toward him. He watched in quiet fascination as the wind tossed her hair and her body moved under a fitted blue dress.

"Let's go to Garcia's," she said. "It's the best."

He let her take charge at the restaurant. She chose the table on the terrace overlooking the bloated river. She ordered on his behalf with the assumption that he, the guy with the questionable Spanish skills, would not know how to order Latin food. He watched her come alive in the fresh air, pushing her sunglasses to the top of her head, eyes glistening, gesticulating madly as she talked. Over ceviche and cerveza, she kept the conversation light and he played along. At some point, she lifted the weight of her hair off the nape of her neck to better feel the breeze. When she leaned forward to reach for a napkin, the deep V-neck of her dress revealed more than she might have wanted—and he remembered everything.

The party.

Champagne.

The woman in the kitchen.

That evening, she'd worn her hair in a knot and was dressed plainly in a black shirt and pants. She'd managed to calm his ex down. And Viviana wasn't a woman who was easily calmed. More importantly, she'd compared him to a shot of rum. He would've gone for whiskey.

No wonder he'd forgotten! That whole week had been emotionally charged. He'd made the decision to move to Miami only minutes after receiving the offer for a lateral move as a partner. He'd acted on his instincts. And when Viv tried to turn a summer thing into a more permanent one, those same instincts told him to nip that in the bud. Still, even during that windstorm, he'd noticed this woman bent over a table, tense over having to pour from a respectable bottle of champagne. The opening of her loose blouse had offered the same gorgeous view as now. How could he have walked away?

Sofia pointed to a pelican perched on a dock, its damp feathers coated in mud. "Poor little guy."

"I have a question for you," he said.

"Yes?"

"How do you like your rum? With Coke, ice or like I like it, neat?"

She went still. "You remember."

"Every little thing." He leaned back in his seat. "You never thanked me for helping out with the champagne."

"I never asked for your help," she said evenly.

"And women wonder why chivalry is dead."

"You weren't being chivalrous. You were *showing off.*"

"Okay," he said. "You got me."

"Just curious. How's your friend?"

"She's fine," he said. "You don't have to worry about her."

She shook her head as if she'd lost all faith in mankind. "You never thanked me for defusing *that* bomb."

He thanked her with a tip of an imaginary hat. "You have my undying gratitude."

She shrugged a slender shoulder. "Just doing my job."

Now he better understood her reticence. "You think I'm a jerk," he said. "A woman cried and you bought the whole act."

"Was it an act?" she asked.

"I think so," he said. "Does that make me a jerk?"

"I don't know what it makes you. I don't know you that well."

He leaned forward. "Let's get to know each other, Sofia. Really well."

She mimicked his move, resting her arms on the table and leaning in. "That's not going to happen, Jon."

"How significant is this 'other' of yours?" he asked.

If he'd taken a second to think, he might not have asked the question, not so bluntly anyway. But now that it was out there, he had to know.

"Well..." She scooped ceviche with a cracker.

"I'm listening." He wiped his hands on his cloth napkin and gave her his full attention.

"We're engaged."

The blow left him winded—and inexplicably angry. "That's pretty significant. Why didn't you say that earlier?"

"That option wasn't on the jury questionnaire. It was a choice between Married, Single or Significant Other."

"You could've penned it in," he said.

She gave him a quizzical look. "For the benefit of the court?"

"You're not wearing a ring," he observed.

She dropped the cracker and drew her hands onto her lap. "I don't wear it every day. It wouldn't be practical. It's really big."

"Oh, is it?" he asked.

He'd hammered every syllable. Then he watched with some satisfaction—no, he watched with life-sustaining satisfaction as color drained from her cheeks. She raised her glass to her lips, took a couple of gulps of beer and once she'd regained her composure, she suggested they leave.

"I don't think there's time for seafood pasta. Maybe we should head back."

"There's always time for seafood pasta."

Their waiter arrived with a fragrant bowl of linguine loaded with shrimp, clams, mussels and calamari. He had to be the luckiest man alive.

There was time for pasta followed by better coffee than they could hope to get at the courthouse snack bar. There was also time for a slow stroll back to his car and for more questions.

"Why don't you tell me more about what you do?" he asked.

"If I thought you'd believe it, I'd say it's all very glam and fun."

"Then tell me how it really is."

"Long hours. Demanding clients. Some days it's a three-ring circus."

"Why do you do it?"

He held open the car door for her. She stopped and gave him a thoughtful answer. "When everything comes together, it's like magic. Then you blink and it's over. You've got to pack up the circus."

"But you know you've made magic."

She smiled and ducked into the car.

Jon drove slowly, which was against his very nature, in an effort to stretch their time alone together. They made it back to the courthouse just in time. His plum spot in the parking lot was taken. He squeezed into a space between a boxy Scion and a sporty BMW.

"Look at that," she said. "We're parked next to each other."

He turned to the Scion.

She poked his arm. "That's what you think of me?"

The BMW then… It was a white convertible with a black cloth top. It suited her. And then it hit him how badly he'd wanted to impress her with his credentials, career and yes, his car. He had to laugh.

"What's so funny?" she asked.

"I really am a show-off."

It didn't take long for her to connect the dots. She opened the passenger door. "Yeah, you are."

He blinked and it was over. The minute they returned to the jury room, she was selected for a panel. He'd swear her eyes clouded with regret. "It was nice meeting you again, Jonathan-Gunther-defense-attorney-single-no-kids."

It was great that she'd memorized his stats, but that goodbye sounded too final. "How can I get in touch with you?"

She shook her head, lifted that huge purse and left the room.

Jon exited the courthouse at three-thirty without having ever been selected for a panel. He'd spent the afternoon in the quiet room replying to emails, but mostly counting the minutes until he could camp out in the parking lot and ambush her. Now he skipped down the courthouse steps and stopped short when seeing from across the street that her car was gone, and his car looked lonely for a friend.

The note tucked under his windshield wiper didn't catch his eye until he'd started the engine. He got out and grabbed it. Two words beautifully penned on the back of his business card in that unmistakable indigo ink: *Thank you.*

Chapter 3

Sofia wasn't clear when chatting had crossed into flirting, or even how he'd roped her in, but here she was, tied up in knots. The man was magnetic—clever, witty and *fun*. When the time had come to leave him, she couldn't pull herself away. Then the case for which she'd been picked was dismissed. She had the choice of leaving early (forfeiting her fifteen bucks) or returning to the jury pool. Her brain opted to leave; the rest of her wanted to rush back into the auditorium to be with him. Although she'd managed to follow the other elated jurors out the door, she couldn't resist leaving something behind. He must think her nuts, going on about her engagement one minute and leaving him a note the next.

She *was* nuts.

Driving in circles, finding her way out of the parking lot, she wondered what had gotten into her. The first time they'd met, she was able to dismiss him pretty fast. But things had been different then. She had really been engaged, and now she was only pretending to be. Not pretending, she reasoned. She and Franco had privately ended their engagement. They simply hadn't gone public with that information yet.

Who was she kidding? Nothing about their situation was simple.

She drummed the steering wheel. What to do now? It was only two thirty. She had a meeting at five. Leila Amis, a Realtor and friend, had recruited her to throw an open house for a new listing in Miami Beach. Part of her business had always focused on providing local Realtors with the services they needed. With the influx of foreign investors, Miami's luxury real-estate market was thriving. Sofia was being offered more and more work. She could head back to her office to start on a concept or...

Was Jonathan Gunther built like a boxer under that suit? Looked like it.

For the love of God, Sofia!

In need of a lifeline, she called Leila, who barely gave her a chance to say hi. "Hey! I know we agreed to meet at the house." Her voice poured through the car speakers. "Any chance you can swing by the agency later to pick me up? My car is in the shop. It broke down on I-95 this morning. They towed it away. It was a mess."

Sofia looked up and around to better situate herself. She was at the junction of I-95, and all she'd have to do was head south to Brickell. "Any chance we can do this now? I've got time to kill."

"In that case," Leila said, "I'm going to put you to work."

Brickell was two things: a trendy neighborhood lined with luxury condo buildings and the center of Miami's financial district, if one in fact existed. Joggers, dog walkers and professionals in business suits mingled on the sidewalks. The afternoon sunlight set the buildings' mirrored surfaces on fire.

Leila and her boyfriend, Nick, ran a boutique real-estate agency from one of the newer buildings. Sofia pulled up and spotted Leila out front chatting with the doorman. In a former life, Leila used to be a pageant queen and it showed in the way she walked. Sofia watched as she approached and elegantly lowered herself into the passenger seat. She wore a fitted cream jumpsuit that flattered her deep brown complexion.

"First stop," she said, "the downtown Hyatt. I have to meet with a client—five minutes, tops. Then we'll head out to South Beach—can't wait for you to see the listing. The photos I sent you don't do it justice. Then maybe we could stop somewhere for drinks? Catch up a little."

Sofia eased back into the slow-moving traffic. "Or we could shop for a new car. Don't you think it's time for an upgrade?"

Leila had been driving the same Mazda Miata for as long as Sofia had known her. She'd won it at a pageant, but her sentimental attachment to the thing bordered on ridiculous.

Leila quickly switched topics. "Took a day off?"

"Nope. Jury duty."

Leila made a face. "How did that go?"

Sofia answered without thinking. "I had a good time."

"At jury duty?"

Sofia scrambled to correct herself. "I had…a good book."

Leila was quiet for a while, messaging clients. They arrived at the Hyatt and Sofia waited in the car, listening to the radio, for at least fifteen minutes. Leila wrapped up her meeting and they headed out to Miami Beach.

On the causeway, Sofia lowered the convertible top. The bay stretched out on either side of the strip. As the breeze tossed her hair, she felt a tinge of excitement. She was eager to visit this house. She'd thought the photos were spectacular and had instantly fallen for the house's modern design and open layout. But Leila was right: there was nothing like touring a house to get a feel for it. Her father owned a construction company and all her life she'd toured homes at various stages of development. Even the most cookie-cutter of homes had a personality. Which reminded her of something. Nick and Leila had been renovating a house in Bayshore for the better part of a year. Some days it was all Leila could talk about.

"How's progress on Barbie's dream house?" Sofia asked, knowing she'd regret it.

"There've been some delays getting permits for the garage," Leila replied. "It's pissing Nick off. But did I tell you about the custom furniture?"

"Many times."

Leila squealed. "I get a sneak peek of the living room furniture tomorrow."

"Good luck sleeping tonight!" Sofia teased.

"I've got a question for you, smart-ass," Leila said. "When's the wedding? Forget car shopping. Why aren't we out shopping for a gown right now?"

"Did my mom put you up to this?" Sofia asked.

"You put me up to this. What kind of maid of honor would I be if I didn't ask?"

Sofia's cousin, Mercedes, was her official maid of honor; Sofia's mother had insisted on it. Leila had agreed to sign on as the de facto maid of honor. But none of that mattered anyway, since there'd be no wedding. If Leila wanted to plan a wedding so badly, maybe she should drop Nick a hint.

"I thought you wanted a summer wedding," Leila persisted. "Summer is around the corner."

"A summer wedding was a dumb idea," Sofia said. "I'd melt in the heat."

"What do you think about Christmas?" Leila asked.

"I'm not thinking, Leila," Sofia said. "I'm focusing on my parents' anniversary party."

That was her go-to excuse, but a lame one. Everyone who knew her knew damn well that she could plan ten major events and a kids' tea party all at the same time.

"When's that again?" Leila asked.

"Next month," Sofia said, tense. "Then I'm free."

"Good."

Leila's phone chimed again. She typed a text message and said, "By the way, a client is waiting for us at the house. I promised him an early look at this property before it hits the market. Oh, and I'm taking Brie to a Heat game next week. It's her birthday. Wanna come? Make it a girls' night?"

Brie was Leila's assistant, who'd been with her through tough times and now, it seemed, really good times.

"Sure," Sofia replied absently. "Girls' night!"

"We're almost there," Leila said. "Head north on Alton."

"Will your client mind my being there?" Sofia asked.

"No, he'll love it," Leila said. "Hotshot lawyer. You know the type."

Sofia shrugged off the cold hand of dread. *Don't be paranoid*, she told herself. Miami was crawling with hotshot lawyers.

"Last house on the block. Pull up to the gate."

They were still some feet away, but Sofia could see the property walled off from the busy street and overflowing with tropical flowers. She let out a low whistle. "It's like an oasis."

"Go ahead and park at the curb behind that Porsche," Leila said. "I don't have the clicker for the gate."

Oh, no, no, no, no, no! Sofia hit the breaks and came to an abrupt stop, sending Leila lurching forward and her purse tumbling to the car floor.

"Hey!" Leila cried.

What were the damn odds? When she'd left the note on the windshield of that same Porsche, the plan was to never see the owner again. She'd made fuzzy choices all day, but on that point she'd been very clear.

"You know what?" Sofia said, trying to buy time.

Leila smoothed her straight black hair. "What?"

"I should go."

"Go where? We've got work to do! I want to hear your ideas for the open house."

"I don't feel so well."

"Have you eaten today?"

At first glance, the Porsche appeared to be sitting empty, but now the driver's door swung open and Jonathan Gunther—all six feet and however many inches of him—got out.

I'm going to lose it today.

"That's my client," Leila whispered. "You're welcome."

Sofia shrunk behind the wheel. With the top down, there was nowhere else to hide. Drivers stuck behind her were honking, and Leila nudged her in the ribs.

"Sofia, you're holding up traffic."

Other than pushing Leila out of her car, what choice did she have? She pulled up to the curb but refused to cut off the engine.

Jon came around to the passenger side and leaned down low. He flashed them the smile of a Viking conqueror.

"Jon," Leila said. "This is my friend Sofia Silva. She's a real-estate event planner. Sofia is planning our open house."

Those brown eyes pinned her in place. "Hi, Sofia. I'm Jon."

Sofia nodded and said nothing.

"She's not feeling so well," Leila explained.

Sofia gripped the steering wheel. When did Leila become such a chatterbox?

"Something you ate?" Jon asked innocently.

"I bet she hasn't eaten all day. This woman lives on coffee." Leila frowned. "I think she should come inside."

"She absolutely should."

Sofia had the feeling of having walked onto the set of a comedy sketch. The best thing, the smart thing, would be to speed off, leaving these two jokers in the dust. And yet, when Jon held open the car door for Leila, and she stepped out and gave him the briefest of hugs, Sofia felt a twinge of…envy.

"You'd be doing me a favor if you stayed," Jon said. "I need a pair of objective eyes."

"Well, good luck with that," Leila said. "Sofia's already in love with the place. She thinks it's an oasis."

Like any true oasis, Sofia thought, it was proving to be an illusion.

"Sofia, are you in love?" Jon asked.

"No. I don't fall that easily."

"Good. I'd hate it if you did."

"And I'd love it if we got around to seeing the house," Leila said. "That's what we're here for. Come on, Sofia! Let's go!"

Chapter 4

While Leila unlocked the gate, Jon couldn't get over his luck. Why were they playing this game? He wasn't sure. Jon was taking his cues from her, and she'd turned white with panic at seeing him again. This told him something: their encounter hadn't been casual. It hadn't been for him and now, obviously not for her, either.

The gate gave way to a lush green space filled with colorful flowers. A compact white house with modern lines and wide glass panels was tucked deep in the yard. Jon paid attention as Leila listed the pros and cons. Pro: the Alton Road location placed it at only a short bike, bus or Vespa ride away from Lincoln Road, the clubs and the beach. Con: the Alton Road location and its legendary congestion and chaos, which turned off most buyers.

"I mean if a kid kicks a ball into the street and chases after it, that kid will get flattened by a Lamborghini," Leila said. "That's all I'm saying."

"Is this your best sales pitch?" Jon asked.

"I'm looking out for your best interests."

A tax attorney at his firm had referred him to Leila's agency. Jon enjoyed working with her. She was patient, never pushy and committed to finding him something reasonable and affordable. They were becoming fast friends.

"What did I tell you about being so ethical?" he teased.

The wide front door was unremarkable except for the

exotic grain of the wood. Jon took hold of the industrial hardware. "I like this."

"I thought you would," Leila said. "This house is made for a man like you."

"Meaning?"

The question came from Sofia who had trailed behind, admiring the spare landscaping as if lifted from the Luxembourg Gardens. Jon loved her curiosity—where he was concerned.

"It's not quite the bachelor pad you need," Leila explained. "But it has the look, you know?"

Jon wasn't looking for a pad, but a sanctuary. He worked long hours and needed someplace comfortable and calm to come home to. He had a good feeling about this house. The street noise was an issue, but the high-impact windows would block out most of it. He didn't have a kid to worry about, and he knew to look both ways before crossing the street, whether or not he was chasing after a ball.

Leila let them in and went ahead, switching on lights and pulling back drapes. Jon waited for Sofia who was, it now seemed obvious, deliberately trailing behind.

"It's been a couple of hours," he said. "Missed me?"

"For the record," she said, stepping up to him, "I didn't know she was meeting you."

"For the record, I know you're not too upset about it." He was over the moon about it. He'd thought she'd slipped away, and had considered asking his firm for the name of the event-planning business that had thrown his welcome party. Which reminded him of something. "Since when are you a real-estate event planner?"

"Since always!" she snapped.

"Come in, guys," Leila said. "Feel free to look around, ask questions."

Most Miami houses looked the same to Jon. A large

main room generally opened to some kind of back patio. This one had clean uncluttered lines, and it was kind of sexy. The floors were the color of porcelain. A glass spiral staircase led to the second floor. What struck him was the wall of windows, two stories high, which framed the yard and pool. Midnight swim, anyone?

Sofia walked past him. "Does it come fully furnished?"

Jon gave the living room furniture a second look. The chocolate leather couch looked delicious. A glass coffee table caught the light of the starburst chandelier hanging above it.

"Look who's suddenly interested in furniture!" Leila observed.

"Just curious," Sofia said.

"The furniture is not included." Leila explained the house was staged for effect.

Then she led them into the kitchen. The narrow space was made bright with pale wood cabinets and strategically placed recessed lighting. Leila pointed out the golden Italian marble counter. "This definitely comes with the house."

"Gorgeous," Jon said. He watched Sofia run a hand over the glossy countertop. The woman was gorgeous.

"You have a good eye," Leila said. "Most men don't."

"Can't take my eyes off it."

Sofia glanced over her shoulder at him and quickly turned away. Her cheeks had that rich wine color he liked so much.

"This is where you'll make breakfast for your women friends," Sofia said innocently. "Since this is meant to be a bachelor pad and all."

"I've got a Keurig," he replied. "They'll get coffee. Or tea."

"Coffee *or* tea? Wow!" Sofia exclaimed. "You must sweep them off their feet."

"I do all right."

"Let's check out the yard," Leila said. "It's killer."

The kitchen opened to the yard with a framed glass door. It seemed to Jon the entire rear facade of the house was glass, a smoky glass that revealed nothing. The yard was modern day tropical. There were some grass and palm trees along the property wall, but mostly a slate-gray tile extended right up to the edge of a long rectangular pool. A "negative edge" pool, as Leila described it. Jon watched Sofia walk over to a canopy daybed and pull back the gauzy white cotton curtains. When drawn tight, he imagined they offered complete seclusion.

Sofia sank into the soft mattress. "Is this included?"

"None of it!" Leila snapped. "None of it is included."

Sofia raised her hands. "Okay! Okay!"

Jon liked their chemistry, or lack thereof. They clearly had a bond that could take a blow or two.

"I'm thinking about a sunset affair," Sofia said. "For the open house, I mean. Sangria at sunset."

"Now you're talking," Leila said.

"Can I come?" Jon asked.

Leila's phone rang. Before answering, she said, "Buy this house and *you* could invite *us* over for sangrias."

Leila wandered off with the phone glued to her ear. Jon joined Sofia at the daybed. He wanted her opinion on the place. Did she like it? Did she swim? Would she come over for brunch? Would she stay the night?

He asked none of those questions, taken aback by her serious expression.

"Isn't this too much house for you?" she asked.

"For me alone, maybe," he said. "Don't you like it?"

"I'm not the one you should ask that question."

"Oh, yes. I forgot," he said. "You're off-the-market."

She got up, crossed the yard to the pool. She stood at

the water's edge, looking down. He joined her there and said the one true thing he could think of.

"I missed you after you were gone."

This time, in her haste to escape him, she nearly fell into the pool. Jon caught her just before she went plunging into the deep end. She clung to him, her hands gripping his shoulders. He could feel her heart.

"I got you," he whispered.

She nodded, as though accepting this as fact.

Leila came skipping back. "That was Nick. He's on his way over. How about we check out the bedrooms? The master suite is sexy."

Chapter 5

Two in the morning and Sofia was smarting over the fact that Jon hadn't remembered her right away. She got out of bed, went into the kitchen and poured herself a glass of water. It had taken him half the day to figure out when and where they'd met. Meanwhile, it had taken her only a few seconds. Her life had changed so drastically since their first meeting, it would have been understandable if she'd forgotten all about him. And yet, she hadn't.

Sofia went back to bed. She crawled onto the wobbly air mattress in her brother's spare bedroom—the very symbol of how much her life had changed. After she'd caught her fiancé sexting with some faceless girl, then finding out that the faceless girl was only one in many, she'd had to move out of their condo in Aventura and in with her older brother, Miguel, who was still in a post-divorce funk.

Although months had passed, Sofia still had nausea when she thought about the night her life had fallen apart, which was often. She'd returned home after a late meeting with a client. The lights of their condo had been dimmed, bringing the sparkling water and city views into focus. The TV was on mute and a welcoming silence flowed through the rooms. She heard Franco moving around in the guest bathroom.

Exhausted, she'd stepped out of her heels, waddled over to the couch and curled up with her favorite throw pillow. The TV remote was on the far side of the coffee table next

to Franco's keys, wallet and phone. She'd stared at the remote, willing it to fly into her hands. When Franco's phone
started buzzing and chiming, her eyes had been too dry
from her failed attempt at mind control to focus on the nude
pic that had popped up in a chain of text messages, small
as a postage stamp. Nonetheless, she'd seen it.

The bathroom door swung open. Franco came out,
chuckling to himself and murmuring in that sexy way that
used to make her hot. "Someone is impatient." He came
trotting into the living room, still dressed for work in a
striped shirt and a pair of black trousers. She thought of
a zillion things to say, but her jaw was clenched tight and
the words jammed in her throat.

Franco froze when he spotted her.

The phone chimed again, this time with a text message
consisting of several emojis, one of which was a peach. And
say what you wanted about Franco, the former high school
football star had impeccable reflexes. He leaped over an
upholstered ottoman and snatched the phone off the table.
Sofia, though, couldn't move. She and Franco had been
adrift for some time, and yet she had not seen this coming. She sat perfectly still while all the love she'd ever had
for the man drained from her heart.

That night, Sofia had driven straight to Leila's place.
Nick had answered the door. "She's at a yoga or meditation class or something."

Sofia checked the time on her phone. It was eight thirty.
"You know what? I'll just go."

She'd felt silly showing up like that. She should've stayed
home and dealt with Franco like an adult. Her phone hadn't
stopped ringing since she'd staged her walkout. It rang then.
She hit the ignore button and silenced the ringer.

Nick gave her a quick once-over. "She won't be long. Come in. I'll open a bottle."

Nick was good, luring her in with the promise of treats. "No, I shouldn't—" Her phone buzzed in her hand, provoking a jolt of anger. The next thing she knew she was screaming at the thing. "Stop calling me!"

Nick's blue eyes flashed. If he was judging her, though, there was no trace of it. He stepped aside and ushered her in. "What are you drinking? White or red?"

"Tequila."

"You got it."

Nick called Leila while pouring from a bottle of Patrón. "Sofia is here…Ten minutes?…Don't worry…I love you."

Sofia sat on a kitchen bar stool. "You guys still say 'I love you' on quick calls?"

She'd known Nick long before he and Leila were a thing. Sofia had worked with him on various projects. But the moment Leila had joined his team, it was clear to everyone that they were head over heels in love. But everyone had expected the infatuation to die down, especially after Nick moved away to New York for a year. And yet, here they were, almost two years later, happier than ever before.

Nick placed a glass before her. "We still do a lot of things."

She took a gulp. The tequila went down smooth, but still she choked on it.

"Slow it down," he said. "What's going on with you?"

"Franco and I…"

Nick raised a hand. He didn't seem interested in the salacious details. "Just tell me it's over."

"It's over." Sofia took a breath. Saying it made it true.

"Good," Nick said.

The two men knew each other. Nick used to stop by Franco's car dealership to check out the inventory. Sofia had always suspected they didn't like each other much. What Nick said next confirmed it. "Sofia, Franco is an idiot."

"No. *I'm* the idiot."

"Why blame yourself?" Nick asked.

"Who else is there to blame?" she cried. "We were in trouble for months, for *years*, and I still forced him to propose."

"You can't force a man to do anything," Nick said. "Besides, Leila said you two were wrong for each other."

"She said that?" Sofia sat up straight.

"Leila admires you," Nick said quietly. "She had a feeling something wasn't right, but trusted you knew what you were doing."

"Is that what you two do, cuddle up in bed and gossip about me?"

Nick shook his head. "Not in bed, no."

Sofia frowned. She and Franco never gossiped. Even if she came home with a hot story, he didn't indulge her.

"Why did you want to marry him so badly?" Nick asked.

Sofia hid her face with her hands and groaned. "We'd been together for so long. Since high school! It was the next logical step."

"Forget logic. It either feels good or it doesn't." Nick took her glass and poured the rest of her tequila down the kitchen sink. "So what are you going to do now?"

"No clue. And you wasted some perfectly good booze."

"If you need a place to stay for a few days or weeks, you're welcome to crash with us."

"I'm heartbroken, not homeless. But thanks."

Leila burst through the door. "Sofia! Why didn't you text me, let me know you were stopping by? I would've skipped yoga." She joined Nick behind the kitchen counter and planted a kiss on his shoulder.

Nick and Leila made a ridiculously attractive couple. The brown-skinned beauty and the blue-eyed Canadian had had their share of problems, but they'd come out on the other side.

"Are you up for dessert? I made rum cake." Leila reached into the liquor cabinet and produced a brown bottle. "With this!"

She held up the bottle of Barbancourt, Haitian rum. Sofia and Leila had roots on either side of the island of Hispaniola. Sofia's dad was from the Dominican Republic and while growing up Sofia had visited frequently. Leila, however, had never been to Haiti. She tried to connect with her culture through food—although, not very successfully.

"Not tonight," Sofia said. "Thanks."

"Where's the camera?" Leila asked Nick. "I want to show Sofia the new photos of the house."

"Maybe now isn't the best time," Nick said.

Leila looked from Nick to Sofia. "Why? What's wrong?"

"Nothing's wrong!" Sofia perked up. "Now is a great time. I'm up for it."

"You sure?" Nick asked.

"Sure, I'm sure!"

Sofia was as surprised by her sudden reversal as anyone. She'd come fully prepared to confide in Leila, but something Nick had said held her back.

She admires you.

That night, she avoided Nick's questioning gaze, as she continued to do for weeks.

Shielding her loved ones from the grim reality also became a priority. The following Sunday, she joined her parents at home for dinner. Her mother had lost some weight, as her cardiologist had recommended, and her floral dress she'd worn to church that morning hung loose on her. A massive heart attack and open-heart surgery had revived her ailing Catholic faith. Anyway, her mother had better news to share.

"Your dad and I want to do something special for our thirty-fifth anniversary. And we want you to organize it."

"Dad wants this?"

The question came from Miguel. Sofia's older brother entered the kitchen and stood before the open refrigerator as he'd done as a teen. It was inevitable. When they were home, they reverted to their most juvenile selves.

Miguel grabbed a can of soda from the fridge. "Knowing dad, he'd rather celebrate with the three *b*'s—beer, Buffalo wings and baseball."

"He wants what I want," Mom said.

"Man! You've got it good," Sofia teased.

"It's a big anniversary," Mom said. She worked a knife through a block of *queso blanco*. "Plus, we've had a rough year."

Sofia relived it all. Those long nights in the hospital when they weren't sure she'd pull through had left them all depleted. Her mother was more of herself now, back at work at the shop and cooking Sunday dinners as usual, but with markedly less stamina. That was what worried Sofia, seeing her diminished that way.

Her mother looked up, wistful. "We need…something. You know?"

"Absolutely," Sofia said.

Nothing was as cathartic as a good old-fashioned party with dinner, dancing and drinks—the whole shebang. It was what the family needed to turn the page.

"Look at this." Her mother handed over her phone, the browser open to a Pinterest page. Sofia reviewed pins of venues, flowers, table settings, themes and dresses. "I'm doing it right this time."

Her parents had eloped at the downtown courthouse. "Doing it right" would likely involve a priest.

"Can you afford all this, Mom?" Sofia asked.

Miguel dropped to the floor and held a plank position. "Can you afford Sofia?"

Her mother returned her attention to the stove, stirring a pan of paella. "I don't buy crazy expensive purses and shoes like *some people* do. I've had the same Coach bag for the last three years and my Camry is a decade old. So, yes, you two, I can afford this."

Sofia let the targeted criticism slide. Her parents worked hard and were financially sound. Her dad owned a construction company. Some years it had flourished, others it flailed. But since Miguel had joined the team, expanding operations and taking risks, business was good. Her mother ran a fabric shop downtown, and business had always been steady. Their house was paid off and their retirement secured, but they hadn't traveled or taken a vacation in decades.

"What's your budget?" Sofia asked.

"Five thousand dollars, and your services are free."

Five grand didn't get you much these days, but her mother didn't have to know that.

"You brag about working magic for your clients. It's time you do the same for your family."

"Yeah, Sofia," Miguel said, mid push-up. "Work your magic."

"Just watch me," Sofia said.

She took out her own phone and pulled up her calendar. "Your anniversary is the first Wednesday in April. We should schedule the party on the Friday or Saturday."

"Saturday."

"That's three months away. We're going to have to hustle. I'll need you to be decisive. No mulling over fabrics and flowers for days. Okay?"

Sofia scrolled through Pinterest, pausing at a pin of a white-and-gold place setting. It was gaudy enough to satisfy her mother's tastes while remaining tasteful.

"I want you and Franco to say a few words at the reception—as a couple."

Sofia lowered the phone. "Why? Isn't that Miguel's job? He's the oldest."

"I'm depressed and divorced." Miguel hopped to his feet. "Haven't you heard?"

"You're *depressing*," Sofia said. "I know that much."

"Leave your brother alone, will you?" her mother scolded. "Not everyone is as lucky as you and Franco. Where's Franco, anyway?"

"Yeah, Sofia," Miguel said evenly. "Where is Franco, anyway?"

She glared at him. "Busy. Work stuff."

At the mention of Franco's name, Sofia's mask had nearly cracked. Her parents would not take the news of the breakup well. They were traditional. A married life was a settled life, in their opinion. Her mother, in particular, had had a hard time with Miguel's divorce and she hadn't even liked his wife. Sofia knew how her mother's mind worked. Her illness and Miguel's misfortune were signs the family was vulnerable, brittle, falling apart. The end of Sofia's engagement would make it clear. Even Miguel, who knew the whole story, and who'd appeared sympathetic when she'd shown up at his door with an overnight bag, didn't seem to be taking it too well now.

Sofia was sixteen when she and Franco met. Franco played ball with Miguel on weekends and could be counted on for Sunday dinner. As a result of their splitting up, the whole family would have to break up with him as well. That was going to be a tough sell.

"Too bad," her mother said. "He loves my paella."

Nobody loved her mother's paella. Did it do the trick at the end of a long day? Sure. Did anyone wake up craving it? No. Was it technically paella? Not even close. Just some yellow rice with peas, peppers and cod tossed in— not necessarily heart healthy, either. Her mother wasn't the fine Latina cook she thought herself to be. In fact, her mother wasn't Latina at all. She was African American. At nineteen, Clarissa Ross fell in love with Antonio Silva, the smooth-talking Dominican boy who'd moved into the apartment down the hall from hers. Ten months later, she was pregnant. They got married and lived happily-ever-after. All that being said, her *mofongo* was off the charts and her chicken potpie was legendary.

"You and Franco represent the future of our family," her mother said. "Can I count on you two to say a few words? Nothing fancy."

"Yeah, Sofia," Miguel chimed. "Nothing fancy. You *and* Franco can handle that."

What was Miguel's problem? And what was she going to tell her mother? Their family had no future? She wasn't that cruel.

That Sunday, after dinner with her family, Sofia sat in her car for a long time thinking about the future. Had she been too quick to toss out the past and Franco with it? She drove to Aventura, back to the home she'd abandoned, where most of her clothes, her comfy pants and her favorite pillow had been left behind. It was time she and Franco had a talk.

He greeted her at the door, looking rumpled and contrite. They sat at the dining table. Franco rushed to apologize.

"None of those women meant anything to me."

Women. Plural. Did he have to remind her that it wasn't just one faceless girl, but legions?

"I never met any of them in real life," he continued. "It was all for play. Something to do when I was bored."

"So, I bored you."

"No," Franco said. "That's not what I meant. Damn it, Sofia. I wish there was a way for me to make it all up to you."

Sofia raised a hand to silence him. That silence stretched on forever. They sat at the table, not speaking, not even looking at each other. Sofia had promised herself that the breakup wouldn't break her. But when finally she tried to speak, her voice buckled and failed. She took a breath and started again.

"We're family," she said.

Franco had been there for her the whole time her mother was in the hospital. He'd shown up early with coffee and returned after work. He'd brought her dinner, a change of clothes, whatever she needed. He ran errands for her dad. He'd been like…a brother.

Franco exhaled with relief. "We *are* family."

"And if you ever need anything, call me."

She stood, ready to leave, but not before retrieving her favorite pillow and packing up her comfy pants.

"That's it?" Franco asked.

Sofia walked over to the hallway closet and pulled out a large suitcase. "That's it."

"I don't want things to end this way," he said.

She turned to face him. "Things are not going to end this way. We're staying engaged for three more months, and then it's officially over. That's what I've come to tell you."

"I don't understand," Franco said.

"My mom is expecting us to make a couple's toast at

her anniversary dinner in April, and we're not going to let her down."

Sofia wheeled the suitcase into the bedroom, pausing on her way to look at Franco alone at the table.

"Don't look so confused," she said. "You wanted a way to make it up to me. This is the way."

Chapter 6

Because Jon had a smart mouth, growing up he got his ass kicked—a lot. Then one day, a cousin told him to bulk up or shut up. If some kids found camaraderie and guidance at a local Y, Jon found the same in a dank basement gym in New Jersey where he started lifting weights. At fourteen, when he left his mother to live with his father, an airman then stationed in Germany, he was taller than most kids and all lean muscle.

A year later, his father transferred to the UK. There Jon followed some older kids to an off-base boxing club where he practiced sparring, mastered drills and generally kept out of trouble. The first time he entered a ring at sixteen, he was a mere featherweight. By the time he returned stateside to attend college at Syracuse, he'd gained muscle and weighed in as a middleweight. He'd won a few fights and earned a scholarship from an intercollegiate boxing association that put a dent in his tuition.

Boxing had shaped his life in ways others couldn't appreciate. His parents had mixed reactions to his newfound passion. His mother was repulsed by it. His father admired it. But they misunderstood it. Boxing hadn't made him a fighter, as his mother feared. It had taught him restraint and self-control. Once word got out that he packed a mean punch, he didn't get into random fights anymore. Kids stopped provoking him. And he could knock their lights out with one right hook, but why would he? It wasn't about showing off. It was about showing skill.

So it made sense that when Jon left Sofia that night, he headed straight to the boxing club to work it all out. The converted warehouse located blocks from the Design District was light years away from the District's freshly painted glamour. The street was dark, pothole ridden and lined with small businesses so precarious they could fold at any time. It seemed that every other shop was holding a going-out-of-business sale. With no signs or markings to call attention to it, the club would have blended nicely with the neighborhood if not for the heavily guarded parking lot filled with sport cars and SUVs. Jon let himself in with a key card, changed in the locker room and headed out to the floor.

Grunting. Slapping. Moaning. Shouts. A few regulars were going at it on the mat. A woman was attacking a heavy bag. An instructor was running a class in the back of the room. "One, two, three, four, five, six, seven, eight, up! Good! Now eight more!" Jon slipped on his headphones and silenced his world. He grabbed a rope and started skipping at a slow pace then at whip speed.

Sofia had to be the most gorgeous liar he'd ever met. He didn't know what she was hiding, but he'd find out. You couldn't succeed in his line of work without the ability to smell deceit. That so-called fiancé of hers…he was calling bullshit. She'd hesitated to mention him. Never once said "we" like his engaged friends did. That was slim evidence, but enough to open an investigation.

A tall blond came to stand right in his field of vision— not the kind of blond that he went for. Andrew Fordham looked disheveled, his tie loose around his neck and his suit jacket crumpled in his hand. He pointed to Jon.

"Lose the headphones. Meet you in the ring in five."

* * *

To a newcomer, Jon and Andrew would not seem evenly matched. Slim and fair, Drew didn't look like much of a threat, but he was lightning fast and landed his punches with accuracy. But Jon's bulk didn't ever slow him down. They danced, circling each other, falling into a rhythm.

"Did you hear?" Drew asked.

Jon ducked, narrowly avoiding his jab. "Hear what?"

"They got Taylor Benson."

Jon had heard. He'd watched the news over breakfast yesterday. The Florida Department of Revenue had announced the arrest of a former pop star turned Miami Beach nightclub owner. Taylor Benson had allegedly failed to turn over to the state one hundred grand in sales taxes collected at his two thriving nightclubs. Drew would be prosecuting the case. Naturally, Jon congratulated his friend before taunting him.

Drew struck, his glove skimming Jon's chin. "Benson is going away for a long time."

Jon went in for the attack, but Drew adroitly ducked away.

"Sounds personal," Jon said. "Let me guess. You got kicked out of one of his clubs?"

"I'm wiping out corruption." Drew circled him. "What have you done this week?"

"I met a woman." Jon hadn't realized it but he'd stopped moving. He stepped back and leaned against the ropes. "I really like her."

"Damn it! You always win!" Drew cried. "Who is she? Anyone I know?"

"I can't disclose that information. Not yet."

Drew let out a low whistle. "That's serious!"

From the floor, one of the trainers shouted at them.

"Hey! If you two sweethearts don't get moving, I'm gonna ask you to step out of the ring."

"You heard the man," Drew said. "Get off your ass. Let's go."

Jon pushed off the ropes and landed his first punch.

Chapter 7

"Check us out." Brie pointed to the reflection in the ladies' room mirror. "We look like a '90s girl band."

Sofia was sandwiched between Leila and Brie at the sinks. In their bright lipstick and little black dresses, they matched. Leila was the pretty one, Brie the wild one and Sofia the surly one who wouldn't make it as a solo artist.

It was a Thursday night and they were gathered at the penthouse of a Brickell high-rise to preview an ambitious new Miami real-estate project. The condominium tower, slated to go up in a few months, would transform the skyline and rival any building in Dubai. It would feature a helipad, a marina and five floors dedicated to amenities. Nick and Leila had come to scope out the competition. Brie had come for the free drinks. And Sofia had come to avoid another night watching TV alone at Miguel's place, although her stated objective was to recruit new clients.

The trio parted ways outside the ladies' room with plans to touch base in one hour or so. Leila joined Nick. Sofia was on her way back to a secluded spot on the balcony where she'd spent most of the evening "admiring the view" when Brie grabbed her by the elbow. She shoved a glass of champagne in her hand. For the first time in Sofia's life, the sight of sparkling bubbles made her sad. Even this event, as glamorous as it was, so glamorous she really should be taking notes (an oyster bar, a vodka tasting station...), had left her indifferent.

"Take a sip!" Brie ordered. "You've been lost in your feelings all night. You need to loosen up."

Brie wasn't so much Leila's assistant as much as the bossy little sister Leila had never had. A pretty girl with deep brown skin, hair that changed seasonally—presently cropped short and dyed blue—and a vivacious spirit, she was always the life of the party. Her birthday was no exception. The fact that her birthday was long over made no difference. They'd celebrated two nights ago at a Heat game, but Brie had claimed the entire week as her own.

Sofia offered the standard excuse. "It's nothing. I've got a headache."

It wasn't a lie. Since her life had turned into performance art, Sofia wasn't her best. She was moody, sluggish, bloated and prone to migraines. To make matters worse, there was no one to blame but herself. She'd cooked up the scheme that now consumed her. There were a million ways she could have ended things with Franco, and she'd chosen the single most complicated one. It was against her nature to lie and plot like this. She was a sharp shooter, direct and honest to a fault. The surprising end of her engagement had drawn out a side of her she did not like.

"This place is crawling with millionaires," Brie said. "You should be doing your thing."

Lately, her thing was to curl up on a couch after work with an assortment of snacks. And since she was on the topic of snacks, Sofia eyed the sushi station with some longing.

Brie nudged her. "That looks delicious."

"Yes, it does."

"Not the food," Brie said.

Sofia followed Brie's gaze out to the center of the room. Jon.

What was he doing here?

She must have uttered the question out loud because Brie answered. "He's our client. We invited him."

Jon was studying the artist renderings of the future building. A saleswoman was working him over. Sofia had it memorized: 10 percent down, 10 percent at groundbreaking, etc. She couldn't believe he'd consider buying a soulless condo in a glass tower all because it had a helipad. With the cheaper units priced in the high nine hundreds, Sofia couldn't justify the expense. What was Leila thinking? Her job was to shield her client from bad choices, not lead him to them.

Jon looked up. They locked eyes. Could he feel her judging him? Sofia took a sip of champagne to wet her throat. As he approached, her cheeks grew hot. This was the reason—the only reason—she'd resolved to avoid him. The physical reaction that he provoked and that she, for some reason, couldn't hide. She looked down at her hand to make sure she was wearing her ring, knowing full well the little diamond solitaire couldn't help. It wasn't kryptonite.

"Help," Jon said. "I need cover. Every salesperson here is out to get me."

"They're targeting young hot professionals," Brie said. "That's you."

Brie was beaming and Sofia envied her freedom to flirt and tease. Sofia envied her freedom, period.

"I think you know Sofia Silva," Brie said.

"I think so, too," Jon said.

From across the room, Leila gestured for Brie to join her. Brie groaned and promised to be back soon. Once Sofia was alone with Jon, he leaned closer and whispered, "Can I tell you a secret?"

She nodded, her temperature rising to an alarming degree.

"I'm starving and I've got to eat. Oysters are not going to cut it."

Sofia laughed, headache and moodiness gone. "There's a sushi station behind you."

Jon glanced over his shoulder and let out a primal moan of satisfaction. "Should I get us something or a whole lot of things?"

"I already ate."

"Wait here," he said. "I'll be back."

A few minutes later, when she was staring at a gorgeous and colorful sashimi platter, she wondered how he knew all the things she liked. She led him to her spot on the terrace where he could sit and eat without balancing a plate on his lap. If it offered them a secluded spot to talk, well, so be it. When he handed her a pair of chopsticks, she reached for it without hesitation and stuffed a rosy piece of salmon in her mouth.

The party chatter swirled around them and a local hotshot DJ had started a set. Then Jon spoke and all that noise faded.

"What's your fiancé up to on a random Thursday night?" he asked.

It wasn't a trick question, but Sofia had trouble with it anyway. She had no idea how Franco spent his leisure time now that they lived apart. "This is a girls' night thing. I'm here with Brie and Leila."

"Except Leila is here with Nick."

"Well…it's also a work thing."

"Something's up with this fiancé," Jon said. "I'm starting to think he doesn't exist."

"Why would I invent a fiancé?" Sofia asked.

Jon drew his brows as if the question required deep thought. "If you needed an alibi, he could provide one."

Sofia couldn't get over how twisted his imagination was. She held up her left hand. "Here's proof."

"Exhibit A," he said, without even glancing at the ring.

She reached for a piece of yellowtail tuna and changed the subject. "What did you make of the presentation? Will you be buying in? Is a million-dollar condo in your future?"

He shook his head. "Not for me. With so much going on, how'd I sleep at night?"

How did he sleep at night? she wondered, now biting into a piece of fresh crab.

"You haven't eaten," he observed.

He was right. She'd had a granola bar for dinner. And now she realized that he hadn't touched the food she'd been wolfing down.

"Why wouldn't you let me get you anything?" he asked.

"Because," Sofia said, "men offer food and women say they don't want food. It's the way it works."

"Like when you order a salad but really want a steak?" Jon asked.

"Speaking of food," Sofia said, "if you do buy a condo, no one will expect you to make breakfast. Those kitchens are so small."

He leaned closer. "What's your obsession with breakfast?"

"Me? I don't even eat breakfast!" she protested. Although she understood why he would think that. "Just some coffee and toast most days."

"Is that another thing women say for no apparent reason?"

She popped a blushing shrimp in her mouth and said nothing.

"I'm not ruling out a house," he said. "That first one Leila showed us was pretty good. It was worth the trouble of making breakfast, don't you think?"

"It was perfect." The open house had gone well and

Sofia knew it wouldn't last very long on the market. She could see it now with its clean design and open airy rooms. She'd loved how the slate-gray hardscape of the yard had yielded to the soft blue waters of the pool. "And so sexy."

"It's no bachelor pad, though," he said. "It felt like a home. Know what I mean?"

"A home for a couple just starting out," Sofia said. "No kids and no plans beyond traveling Europe."

"Do they own a dog, this couple?"

Sofia thought about it. A small and sturdy dog felt right. "Sure."

"Say 'sexy' again."

He looked at her, light brown eyes glowing…rum pouring into her open hands. Sofia forgot herself. She held Jon's gaze, knowing full well what her eyes revealed.

Brie found them. She came rushing over and plopped down on the seat between them. "There you are! I need cover from my bosses. They don't know when to quit."

"They're pros," Jon said.

"Well, I need a break," Brie said. "And another drink."

"Come on," Jon teased. "You're young. You can handle it."

And so they carried on. But very soon Nick and Leila joined them, and all four talked around Sofia. They made plans to meet with Jon over the weekend to show him options beyond million-dollar properties in glass towers with helipads. Sofia rested her chopsticks and told herself she wasn't jealous. Only moody, sluggish and bloated. Also, her headache had returned.

Then it was time to go. "Come, Sofia," Leila said. "If we don't leave now, there'll be a line at the valet."

Jon stood and thanked her for keeping him company. They exchanged a brief good-night hug. As she followed Leila toward the elevators, Sofia chanced a look over her shoulder. Jon was speaking to Brie, who'd stayed behind, his back to Sofia. With her very next step, Sofia toppled head first into a ditch of disappointment.

Chapter 8

A petite brunette was taking a selfie on the balcony overlooking the beach. Sofia had spotted her from the front door and knew she'd walked in on one of Miguel's dates. He'd joined a service and made dating his part-time job. This was the third time in a week. She was tired of coming home to sideways glances and hushed promises that she wouldn't "be in the way." Sofia said hello, ducked into her room for her gym bag and left.

After his divorce, Miguel had bought a condo on a private floor of a Sunny Isles Beach hotel. This way he enjoyed world-class amenities without having to leave home. More and more, Sofia relied on those same amenities. To avoid crashing her brother's dates, she grabbed dinner at the restaurant off the lobby or worked out at the wellness center.

Tonight, after a vigorous ballet barre class, she found herself alone in the sauna with a very handsy couple. Sofia took a seat on the teak bench and closed her eyes, trying to block out the lovers. Still, their whispered words and muffled laughter reached her. Her heart in knots, she walked out, changed into a bathing suit and headed to the pool.

The infinity-edge pool located on a terrace overlooking the city was deserted. Sofia waded into the cool water until it reached her shoulders. This time when she closed her eyes, it wasn't to block out the world but to take it in.

Lovers.

The water pushed and pulled at her, tugged her limbs and applied soft pressure to her belly. She hadn't been touched in months. What she'd give to be kissed. She thought about Jon for the hundredth time that day. Two weeks had passed since she'd seen him. Was he a good kisser? He was so strong—how would it feel to be in his arms? What kind of lover was he? Would his talk be as frank and direct as in everyday life? She worried she might never find out. She had four weeks of her fake engagement to go. Even then, she couldn't fly into Jon's arms. Every woman's magazine had recommended time. Time to regroup. Time to heal. Time to put herself first. She owed herself that much.

Later that night, Miguel left with his date for a club, and Sofia had the condo to herself. She posted a photo to her company's blog, then logged into her personal email account. Some of her friends were planning a weekend getaway. The email chain's subject line was: Are you in???????? Nope. Sofia shut her laptop. She was definitely out.

She was settled in front of the TV in the living room with a bowl of popcorn when the front desk called to say that Leila Amis was in the lobby, asking to come up.

Busted!

Sofia held the phone to her chest and racked her brain for excuses. What could she possibly say?

Moments later, Leila walked through the door, tossed her purse onto the couch and asked, "What are you drinking?"

"What makes you think I'm drinking anything?" Sofia replied defensively.

Leila looked around, taking in the darkened living room illuminated by the blue light of the TV and the city lights twinkling in the distance. "What makes me think you're sitting here alone drinking? I don't know. I just do."

"How about some white wine?" Sofia had a bottle of Pinot Grigio in the fridge—but she hadn't opened it yet. "I'll pour you a glass."

"Thanks. Be generous."

Leila stretched out on her couch as if waiting for a therapy session to begin. Sofia handed her a glass and sat on the ottoman beside her. "What brings you by?"

"I was showing a condo in your building—your old building—when I thought I'd pay you a quick visit."

Sofia nodded, and adjusted the tie of her bathrobe. "You saw Franco."

"He suggested I come here," Leila said. "Imagine that."

"I'm just keeping Miguel company," Sofia muttered.

"Where is Miguel?" Leila asked.

"He'll be home soon," Sofia replied. Her voice was thin.

Leila narrowed her eyes at her. "How long do you need me to play dumb?"

Sofia looked at Leila for a long while. She should've known she couldn't hide this from her. Leila wasn't her oldest friend, but they'd quickly grown close. It was proof that a true connection did not require years to mature. Sofia had been feeling so miserable and isolated lately that maybe it was time she opened up to someone.

"Franco and I broke up."

"Ah!" Leila sipped her wine. "I'd ask what went wrong, but I already know. You two were just wrong for each other."

"So Nick has informed me."

"Nick knows about this? You told him?"

"That night I showed up at your place and you were at yoga."

"That was months ago, Sofia!"

"I know."

Leila was bewildered. "And he never said anything."

"I swore him to secrecy," Sofia said.

"Why is this even a secret?" Leila asked. "So you broke up. So what?"

"I haven't told my parents yet."

"You think I'd tell them?"

"No, no!" Sofia took a breath and started again. "I went over there to tell you and I lost my nerve. You and Nick looked so happy, so perfect together, and I was feeling..."

Leila's over-the-top happiness had made her unhappiness difficult to manage. That was the petty truth.

"We're happy, but we're not perfect," Leila corrected.

"You're pretty close."

Nick and Leila the super couple was super annoying, but true love was like that. It excluded friends and made haters out of strangers. Sofia understood this and wanted the same for herself. The kind of love that made others want to run and hide. What she'd had with Franco was a facsimile of love.

Sofia got off the ottoman and joined her friend on the couch. Leila rested her feet on her lap. She wore black pumps with a slender heel.

"Love the shoes," Sofia said. "Manolo?"

Leila shook her head; a lock of black hair fell over her eyes. "Prada."

"Nice." Sofia was a Jimmy Choo girl herself.

"I didn't think Nick and I had secrets," Leila said.

Sofia moaned. "Oh, God. This is my fault."

"No, it's not," Leila said. "Sometimes I get the feeling he's hiding something. He's been acting so weird. Has he told you anything?"

"He hasn't. It's not like we're sitting around, brushing each other's hair and swapping secrets."

Leila laughed. "What are you going to do? Live here forever?"

Sofia hadn't thought past the anniversary party. After that, she really was free. Then what?

"Maybe I'll buy a place," Sofia said. "Maybe I'll hire you. Is that house on Alton still available?"

Sofia had asked the question as if the answer didn't matter.

"We got an offer, but the financing is fishy," Leila said. "Jon didn't bite. Can't really blame him now that I think about it. It's big for one person."

"He hasn't made a move?" Sofia asked, nonchalant as all get-out.

"Nope," Leila said. "I haven't heard from him for days. He canceled our last two appointments."

"Ah."

"Do you want to stay in this neighborhood?" Leila asked. "Because there are some exciting things happening in Brickell."

For once in her life, Sofia wasn't looking for excitement. She was feeling like a fraud, lying and pretending. She wanted calm and peace, and some downtime to reconnect with her true self.

And she wanted to know what Jon was up to.

Chapter 9

The week before her parents' anniversary party, Sofia met with her mother for lunch as she would with any client before the big day. They had agreed to meet at Gesu, the oldest Catholic church in the city. It sat at a busy downtown intersection. Its salmon facade was highly visible. Some referred to it only as "the pink church." Located steps from her shop, the church offered her mother a calm retreat on busy days. Her parents would renew their vows there, and later entertain fifty close family and friends at the nearby Intercontinental Miami. The next day, they'd take off on a three-week tour of Italy.

It was Friday and the midday mass catered to the faithful few. They came in office attire and rushed back to their desks as soon as mass was done. Sofia arrived just as the priest raised his arms and said, "Go in peace." Her mother, however, wouldn't leave without first kneeling before the altar to better launch direct missile prayers.

"Couldn't you have come a little earlier?" her mother scolded. They made their way out of the shady opulence of the church to the bright, boisterous city sidewalk. Her mother handed a dollar to a homeless man on the corner. He said thanks and called her "a doll."

"You need prayer in your life," her mother continued.

"Aren't you praying for me?" Sofia asked. "Isn't that what moms do?"

"You're a grown woman. And I can't do all the heavy lifting, not anymore."

The last jab was a reminder of her failing health, a reminder Sofia didn't need.

They stopped at her mother's shop, named simply Clarissa's Fabrics. The storefront window displayed lace, velvet and sequins on sixties-era mannequins. Inside, rows and rows of fabric bails were stacked from floor to ceiling. Cotton. Silk. Crepe. Polyester. The glass showcases held lace trim and even feathers by the yard. Sofia had grown up behind the counter, doing odd jobs. Her duties ranged from sweeping up scraps to counting the cash drawer. She learned all the ways to run a successful business during the good times and keeping it afloat during the hard times. Her mother had had the same two employees for a decade. Sofia chatted with them while her mother went to retrieve the "anniversary binder" from her office in the back of the store. Then, finally, they went to lunch.

Gigi's, a popular Italian restaurant, was overflowing with guests. They settled for a sidewalk table. Over eggplant parmesan and through a haze of gas exhaust, they went through the binder tab by tab.

"See if the florist will have circus roses," her mother said. "I've ordered special ribbon to match. That burnt orange color is very tricky."

"I don't have to double check," Sofia replied. "I've worked with this florist many times. They're reliable. And they have ribbon."

"You just never know."

"*I* know."

"Don't be so stubborn. You're like your father."

"I am not stubborn. I'm sure."

"Ask if we can add a few wild orchids to the bouquet. I've seen it done and it's lovely."

"Orchids? Really, mom?"

What her mother didn't realize was that booking the up-scale restaurant at the Intercontinental had burned through the budget. Sofia had had to pull favors like never before for the upgraded menu, premier floral arrangements and the Spanish guitar soloist her mother had so badly wanted. If the woman added one more thing, just one more thing, Sofia was going to snap.

"Part of my job is to keep you on budget," she said.

Her mother shrugged, resigned. "Okay. No orchids."

The waiter cleared their plates. While they waited for the check, her mother said she looked tired. "Late night last night?"

"Yes, but not like you think. I had an open house in Pinecrest."

"Don't you and Franco go out anymore?" her mother asked.

"We go out plenty," Sofia said.

"When couples settle down, they sometimes lose interest in the things that brought them together in the first place."

"Franco and I don't have that problem."

"Good. We should start planning the wedding soon. Or is he dragging his feet?"

"No one is dragging anything."

"I told you not to move in with him, but you didn't listen. You know what they say about the milk and the cow, right?"

"I'm not a cow."

"I didn't raise a cow," her mother said. "As soon as we're done with this anniversary party, we're working on your wedding. No more excuses."

"Who's making excuses?"

"You cousin Mercedes called last week. Even she wants to know what's the hold up."

Sofia scoffed at that. "She just wants the-maid-of-honor spotlight that you'd promised her."

"And you should want the bride spotlight. That's how it should be."

Sofia looked up at the open skies and launched a missile-powered prayer to the heavens for self-control. *Honor thy mother and father. Honor thy mother and father.* From across the street something—someone—caught her eye.

In what could only be described as the hipster's *cafeteria* with chalkboard walls and wood-crate tables, men in business suits were gathered at the counter. One of those men was Jon, and he was looking at her. Their eyes met just before a container truck stopped at the corner light and walled him off.

Sofia blacked out for a second, realizing that she was trapped. Her mother had an inane ability to see through her; she'd see the butterflies fluttering wildly in her chest.

"This was fun, Mom," Sofia said hastily. "I've got to get back to work."

Her mother stood and gathered her things. "*I've* got to get back to work. *You've* got to stay and settle the bill. The waiter has your card."

"Shit!"

"Language!" Her mother planted a kiss on her forehead. "Now before I go, can I expect you and Franco on Sunday?"

"Yes."

"You *and* Franco?"

"*Yes.*" Sofia hissed the blatant lie.

Her mother left the table, slowly rounding the corner. With her departure, Sofia's dread lifted, giving way to a rush of excitement. Traffic picked up and the truck pushed forward. The waiter still hadn't returned with her credit card. Sofia didn't bother looking across the street. Jon wouldn't be there.

She waited.

"Mind if I join you?"

That deep voice… The hairs on the back of her neck rose to it. She pointed to the chair her mother had vacated and watched him get settled. He was a feast for the eyes, and at that moment, he was all hers to enjoy.

The waiter returned with Sofia's card and receipts. Seeing how the landscape had changed, he asked, "Will there be anything else?"

"Two espressos," Jon said. "Make mine a double."

This woman had made Jon a believer in the power of positive thinking and every other New Age doctrine floating out there. It had been weeks since they'd run into each other, and he couldn't get her out of his mind. The impromptu coffee break had been an attempt to clear his head. He'd spotted her at the restaurant table right away. He guessed she was related to and had a lot of affection for her older lunch companion. She'd looked relaxed and happy, despite the heated conversation. He hadn't planned on interrupting, but then she'd spotted him, too.

Her solemn expression made him want to tease her. "Three times is enemy action, Sofia."

"What does that mean?" she asked.

"You show up wherever I go," he said. "Now even my favorite coffee shop."

"You think I'm stalking you?" she asked.

"I hope you are," he replied.

"I'm not at your favorite anything," she said. "I'm at an Italian restaurant, wrapping up lunch with a client and *you* ambushed *me*."

"Ambush?" The waiter returned with their orders, and he reached for a packet of sugar. "That's an ugly word. We're friends having coffee."

"Is that what you do all day? Hang out at the corner *cafetería*?" she asked. "Shouldn't you be in court getting some crook off the hook?"

"'Crook Off the Hook' is a great title for a kid's book," Jon said.

She smiled. He felt as if he'd scored.

"You're on my turf," he said. His office building soared over the surrounding strip malls; he pointed to it.

She lifted the espresso cup to her lips. Apparently, she took her coffee black. Jon was impressed.

"My mother's fabric shop is around the corner," she said. "And it's probably been there a lot longer than that glass tower. So you're on my turf."

To Jon, that was actionable intelligence. The neighboring shops were modest mom-and-pop operations with longer half-lives than the trendiest restaurants. This added a new element to her profile, a profile that he'd been privately sketching since they'd met. Sofia had working-class roots. It explained her no-nonsense toughness. Under the veneer of style and glamour, long lashes and red lacquered nails, she was hardworking and enduring.

He stirred his coffee. "This client, is she your mother?"

She nodded. "Yes."

"Where's your so-called fiancé?" he asked. "Shouldn't he join his future mother-in-law for lunch?"

"My *fiancé* is working," she said.

She rested her left hand on the table between them, diamond ring on display. This was the second time she'd shoved the thing at him—and for the record, it wasn't that big.

"I never see you with him."

"We're engaged," she said, irritated. "Not Siamese twins."

"You never talk about him."

"I talk about him plenty," she said. "Maybe not as much as you do."

"When we're engaged, I never want you to shut up about me."

Her smile blew him away. "I think there's something wrong with you."

"You may be right."

"How's the house hunt?" she asked.

He finished his coffee before answering. "My heart isn't in it."

"Leila says there's an offer on the house."

"Our house?" he asked.

They shared a look of regret, the truth evident. The house they'd both loved was slipping away.

Jon tried steering the conversation to a cheerier topic. "Why has your mother hired you?"

"I'm planning my parents' anniversary party," she answered. "Thirty-five years."

"Congratulations," he said. "My parents were married for all of two years."

Her gaze raked over his face. They were venturing into murky territory now. He rarely talked about his family. And yet, he now told her how his parents had gotten married when his mother was three months pregnant and divorced before he was potty-trained. His dad had sought the divorce. He'd enlisted in the air force, wanting to be free. At fourteen, Jon had packed up and followed him to Europe.

"If my brother had to pick a side, he'd pick my dad," she said. "I think it's natural for boys."

"I didn't pick a side," he said. "I picked a lifestyle."

He had longed for adventure. New places to discover. New people to meet. His life in New Jersey had seemed small. His dad had been stationed all over the country and around the world. Each postcard he'd received from him had fueled Jon's imagination. When his mother married a middle school math teacher, he took off, joining his father in Germany. Soon thereafter, they transferred to the UK.

"I've never lived anywhere but Miami," she said. "I would love to travel more. Maybe live in Spain a few years."

"You'd miss your family," he said.

"Do you miss yours?" she asked. "You're here on your own."

"I don't think any of them miss me," he said. "They're used to not having me around."

His parents didn't expect to see him very often, not anymore. His mother was well settled with her new family. Since he'd opted out of that family at fourteen, it seemed wrong to request reentry at thirty-two. And after his dad had retired from the military, he bought an RV and continued his adventures, sending postcards as per his custom.

"I can't imagine that. You're so…"

He leaned closer, noticing the flecks of copper in her eyes and the caramel locks of hair. "What am I, Sofia?"

After a slight hesitation, she said, "You know what you are, Jon."

The waiter approached with the dessert menu. "The tiramisu is the house specialty. Want to give it a try?"

Jon was about to ask for the check when Sofia said, shyly, "I'd like to try. How about you?"

He recognized the olive branch before him. She was offering dessert—and friendship.

One hour later, they promised to run into each other by accident again soon. They shared a quick hug and parted ways. In the brief moment he held her in his arms, Jon felt a stab of longing.

Jon had worked as a federal prosecutor prior to joining the Virginia branch of his firm. He'd jumped at the chance to fly to Miami in the dead of winter to help with a case. Some had encouraged him. "You'll love it! The weather this time of year…perfection!" Others weren't so positive. "You'll hate it. So unprofessional! The staff is rude. And the way they dress!"

The weather was perfect, particularly when compared to the arctic conditions he'd left behind in Virginia. The downtown Miami office of the pedigreed law firm was in fact the most unprofessional setting he'd ever worked. Accustomed to conservative work cultures where rules and traditions were strictly observed, the Miami office's loose atmosphere had surprised him.

Was the staff rude? Yes. Absolutely. But their salty sense of humor was just his thing.

Was the dress code observed? No. "There's your dress code right there." A partner in a Hawaiian shirt said on his first day, pointing to a three-piece suit hanging from a hook behind his door.

Was half the office chatting it up in Spanish over Cuban coffee every afternoon at two? Yes, and it didn't take long for him to join in.

One evening before leaving for the day, the receptionist said, "You should transfer down here. You fit in."

Jon knew the twenty-year-old was right. He'd been feeling uprooted for a long while. Fate had led him home.

Meeting Sofia again and again and again…that, too, seemed the design of fate.

Jon walked the few blocks to his office building and stepped into the cool lobby. He had the strange feeling of a door slamming shut behind him.

Once in his office, he got Leila on the phone.

Chapter 10

WHERE ARE YOU???

This was Sofia's tenth text to Franco with no response. The guests were seated. The priest, soloist and organist were ready and waiting. And still no word from Franco.

A day ago, she'd stopped by the dealership to drop off his boutonniere. He'd had good news and bad news. "I leave for Costa Rica on Sunday. These last few months have been stressful. I need to get away."

"All the way to Costa Rica?" she asked.

He grinned. *"Pura vida."*

"So they say."

If the past months had been stressful, she'd designed it that way. She'd wanted him to suffer. And yet today it gave her no joy. She eyed him from head to toe. If her mother had seen him, she'd say he looked thin. Then she'd blame him for skipping Sunday dinners for weeks in a row. "How long will you be gone?"

"A couple months," he replied. "Pike will run things."

Steve Pike ran the used car division. Franco managed new car sales. Still, leaving him in charge of the whole dealership for *months*? That was not a thing she could do. She and Franco had very different managerial styles. Sofia didn't micromanage, but she stayed on top of things. Franco had a laissez-faire attitude, and as a result the business had suffered some losses and been audited twice.

"What's the bad news?" she asked.

"The condo. I planned on paying you back for all the upgrades, but I'm going to need a little time. I'm kind of cash poor."

Sofia hadn't even thought about it. The condo had belonged to Franco's parents. They'd passed it on to him when they'd moved to Boston to be close to relatives—a move Sofia had never understood. Over the years she'd spent money on renovations, tailoring the space to her tastes. She'd renovated the kitchen, splurged on a custom closet and replaced the carpet with hardwood.

"Don't worry about it," Sofia said, adding quickly, "for now."

"Thanks." Franco picked up the boutonniere still in its box and gave it a rattle. "Don't worry about tomorrow. I'm ready. I've picked up my suit from the cleaners and everything."

Sofia nodded, her throat tight. This was goodbye. He'd been a fixture in her life since her teenage years and she realized with some panic that she was scared of a future without him. She could be imagining things, but he looked just as scared.

"Sofia, you were my best friend *and* my first love," he said. "I need you to know that."

Now it looked as if her best friend and first love had stood her up. Fabulous.

The limo pulled up to the curb. Miguel, looking like a new man in a blue Hugo Boss suit, came out of the church. "Move it!" he said, and rushed past her down the steps.

Sofia put away her phone. It was time.

Ordinarily, Sofia found the church's interior oppressive with its statues of saints staring down in judgment. But that afternoon, sunlight touched all the gold accents and the space glowed. Sofia pushed Franco out of her mind, swallowed her rancor and focused on the ceremony. Her mother was radiant in a caramel lace dress. Her father looked distinguished in a tuxedo. Her parents held hands and promised to love each other for the rest of their lives to swelling organ music. There was no doubt in anybody's mind that they would. The matter had been settled thirty-five years ago. Her parents loved each other. The priest in his robe wouldn't make that love any more sacred. Sofia was resigned that she, and maybe even Miguel, might never find that type of love.

Later, at the Intercontinental, Sofia and Miguel welcomed the guests with a toast to the future of their family. They managed to do it without the assistance of her fiancé or his wife, and the sky did not fall. Soon after, her mother made a big to-do of presenting Sofia with her bouquet made of roses *and* orchids. Then she grabbed Sofia by the elbow and dragged her out to the atrium off the hotel lobby. There, in private seclusion, she let Sofia have it.

"Where's Franco?" she demanded. "Don't lie."

Sofia was exhausted. She couldn't come up with a lie if she tried. As far as she knew, Franco had fallen off the earth, or taken off to Costa Rica.

"Okay, Mom. Here's the truth."

Sofia's phone buzzed in her hand. The truth would have to wait. Franco was calling.

Tax fraud.

At two in the morning, Sofia and Franco were arguing—like old times. Only this time it was over the phone. Her parents had insisted Sofia leave the party to be with him. She'd drawn a bright line there. "I've worked really hard to make this event beautiful and memorable for *you*. So help me God, I'm not leaving."

Her parents had backed down. Still, they insisted on a full report in the morning or they threatened not to leave for their trip to Italy. Franco, released on bail, didn't seem to think the situation was all that serious.

"They caught wind of my travel plans, thought I was skipping town," he said. "They jumped the gun."

Sofia noted his tone. It was as if the arrest putting a dent in his travel plans was the most disturbing thing.

"*Were* you skipping town?" she asked.

"No! Can't say for sure what this is all about. I gave the auditor all the information she asked for."

It all had to do with state sales taxes. As a small business owner, all Sofia knew about the state sales tax was that you *had to pay it*.

"I didn't do anything wrong." Franco assured her again he hadn't broken any laws. "You've got to believe me."

She believed him. He was a lot of things, but he wasn't a crook.

"I'm going to need a good lawyer, Sofia," Franco said. "Pike's lawyer seems shady to me."

That was no surprise. Pike himself had always seemed shady to Sofia.

"But maybe Luis knows someone."

Franco's cousin Luis was an ambulance chaser. Who could he possibly know?

"Or maybe I should use a referral service? What do you think?"

"I know someone," Sofia said.

She also knew she'd live to regret having said it.

Early Monday morning, Jon's assistant came into his office with a stack of files.

"I booked your flight to Atlanta," Alex said. "Last flight out next Tuesday."

Jon lowered his binoculars and turned away from the window. "Do me a favor. Look up a yacht called *Prize Fighter*. I love that name."

Jon could see the impressive vessel from his desk and it had drawn him to the window. He was determined to know who owned it.

As he went on with the serious business of the Google search, Alex casually mentioned Sofia. "You have a new client inquiry from a Sofia Silva. She called this morning asking for a meeting. I told her you weren't taking new clients, but she said she's a friend." With a chuckle, he added, "They all say that."

Sofia reaching out? Now that was news to lift a man's sails.

"Did she leave a number?" Jon asked.

"Yes. I can get her on the phone for you," Alex said. "But first, you're going to love this. *Prize Fighter* is owned by movie director—"

"Never mind that! Get me the number."

By the time Alex had made it to the door, Jon had a better idea. She'd called his office and gone the professional route, requesting a "meeting." He'd play along. "You know what? Call her back. Set up the meeting."

"What time?"

"Any time. Right now."

"But don't you have—"

"This is a priority."

Alex returned in five minutes. "She'll be here at eleven with Mr. Francisco Ramirez."

Holy crap! This was an *actual* meeting.

Alex reminded him of an upcoming conference call. While Jon motored through his morning, Sofia was never far from his mind. Nothing lessened the thrill that she'd sought him out. Needed him. And when she arrived at his office dressed as if for a funeral in a plain black dress and black pumps, he was confident he had the upper hand. Jon watched her take in the large windows framing the bay and the bookcases lining the wall behind his desk. When their eyes met... Thunder.

He nodded. *I've missed you, too.*

Jon knew instinctively that the man who trailed behind her, this Francisco Ramirez, was the so-called fiancé. Here they were, all gathered on what could only be labeled his turf.

Jon set a cordial tone. "Let's have a seat."

He led them to the seating area under the window. Sofia sat next to Ramirez on the leather couch, and Jon sat opposite them. She thanked him for agreeing to the meeting on such short notice and for taking the case.

Jon addressed the fiancé. He had to make a few things clear. "I haven't agreed to represent you, Mr. Ramirez. If I can't help, I'll be sure to direct you to the right person for the job."

From the corner of his eye, he saw Sofia's expression darken. Before she could say anything, Jon added, "Either way, you've come to the right place. So why don't you tell me what the issue is."

As it turned out, the issue was plain: the alleged withholding of state taxes collected on used car sales. Why people thought they could get away with crap like that was beyond him. The DMV collected data on every car sold in the state.

"Can you help him?" Sofia asked.

"Not personally, no." He was currently representing an investment firm in a fraud case with millions at stake. That was his speed. "But I have someone on my team who'd be perfect for this case."

The associate that he had in mind was fresh out of law school but, by all accounts, brilliant.

Sofia sat stiffly, her hands gripping the edge of the couch. And, wait one second! She wasn't wearing her ring. Today of all days. Interesting.

"And when will we meet him?" Ramirez asked.

For a second there, Jon had forgotten all about him. "*Her* name is Stephanie Conwell. I'll have my assistant check her availability. She might be able to take a meeting right away."

Jon left them alone. He called Stephanie from Alex's desk to get her up to speed and arrange the meeting. When he returned, they were as he'd left them, sitting in silence and staring straight ahead.

"You're in luck. Ms. Conwell is available," Jon said. "Alex will accompany you two to her office."

Ramirez hopped to his feet. "Okay. Let's go, Sofia."

"I'll stay here," she said.

Ramirez looked dumbfounded. "But don't you want to—"

"No."

Jon looked to one, then the other. "I'll give you two a minute to talk."

"No, don't!" Sofia said.

Her pleading tone grabbed Jon by the heart.

"It's your office," she said. "You shouldn't have to leave."

Ramirez hesitated. "Okay," he said.

As soon as he was gone, Jon joined Sofia on the couch. They had plenty to talk about.

Chapter 11

Alone with Jon, Sofia steeled herself against the difficult conversation ahead. In coming here, asking his help, she knew she'd owe him an explanation. Jon was smart, observant and had surely picked up on the tension between Franco and herself. He'd have questions and she owed him the truth.

"I like you in color," he said.

Naturally, he'd start with a disarming one-liner. Sofia looked down at her strict black dress. It was the most conservative thing she owned, and she had wanted to look serious.

"Sorry to disappoint you," she said.

"That's not possible," he replied. "I have some questions."

She nodded. "I'm ready."

"Do you two have any financial ties? Have you received any direct funds from him or anyone associated with him? Do you know the pedigree of any money you've received?"

"Pedigree? Jon, please!" Sofia cried. "Our businesses are completely independent."

"Your businesses, sure. But you two are a couple. Do you have any joint accounts? Has he made any deposits into your personal accounts? If there's any comingling of funds—"

"We're not a couple," Sofia said flatly. "There's no comingling of any kind."

The air in his stylish office grew still. Sofia stared at the tips of her shoes, her heart pounding against her ribcage.

"Since when?" he asked, the lawyerly tone replaced by something softer.

Sofia let out all the breath in her lungs. "A few months now."

"You're saying I've been right this whole time," he said. It wasn't a question, but Sofia answered yes anyway.

"Why would you do that to me?" he asked.

"I had my reasons."

"Could you share them?"

"A year ago, my mother had a massive heart attack." That was how it had all started, with her mother, the ox of the family, suddenly vulnerable and sick. "She had open heart surgery and for a while, we thought she was going to die."

"Sofia…" Jon said.

"She made it through okay. Then Miguel got divorced. It had been a long time coming, but my mother took it hard. The doctors had warned us against depression. It's common during recovery. Miguel's divorce likely had nothing to do with it. Still, she took it hard."

Jon was listening, head low. Sofia continued. "So when things fell apart with Franco—"

"You kept the news of your own breakup from her," Jon said.

"From her and everyone."

"How does that make sense, Sofia?" he asked.

"I had an exit plan."

"I'd love to hear it."

She told him about the anniversary party on Saturday, and how she and Franco were supposed to toast to the future of their family and then promptly cut all ties with each other.

"And Ramirez agreed to this?"

Ramirez had no choice, Sofia thought. But she couldn't imagine Jon agreeing to anything like it.

"So this party for your parents," Jon continued. "How did it go?"

"He never showed," Sofia said. "He'd been arrested."

"Now what?"

"Now my parents are all full of concern for him."

"And so are you," Jon said. "You're helping him find a lawyer."

"He's not just my ex, Jon," Sofia said. "He's an old family friend and he came to me for help. What was I supposed to do?"

Walking away wasn't an option, not with her parents calling for updates every few hours. And soon, she expected his parents to join the chorus. This way, at least, she could assure them that Franco was settled with a decent lawyer before washing her hands of the whole thing.

"You could've given him my number and sent him off," Jon said. "And you could've not worn that dress."

Again with the dress! Sofia turned to confront him. "You really hate this dress, don't you?"

"I really do," Jon said. "Are you going to tell your parents the truth and cut this guy loose?"

"As soon as they get back from Italy."

She explained it was her mother's dream to visit the Vatican. The woman deserved to enjoy her trip. Her answer didn't satisfy him. He waited, eyes level, for something more.

"I'm sorry I lied to you," Sofia said.

Jon fell silent, and Sofia grew worried. He was such the talker; his silence wasn't natural.

"None of this has been fun for me, Jon," she said. "Meeting you was the one highlight of these past months."

He tilted his head and looked at her a long while. Then he said, "You know what you need?"

"A time machine so I can go back to when we first met and start over?"

"That or a cup of tea," he said.

"Tea? Like chamomile tea?" she asked.

"Like breakfast tea with milk and sugar." He got up and extended a hand. "Come with me."

Sofia let him help her off the couch. Her hand felt cold when he let it go. She followed him out of the office and down the hall to a break room where a few of his colleagues were chatting. He said hello and introduced her as a friend. Then he chose two Keurig cups of English breakfast tea from a bin. He worked quietly, preparing two cups of tea, milk and sugar and all.

"I can't believe what I've just witnessed here," one woman said, bewildered.

"Settle down," Jon said. "It's only tea."

"You've never made us tea!"

This reproach came from an older man in a Hawaiian shirt. Sofia liked the offbeat office atmosphere. She could see how Jon fit in. This morning, she couldn't decide whether she was genuinely helping Franco find a lawyer or looking for an excuse to see Jon in his element. Both were true.

"Maybe if you asked nicely," Jon said.

"I'll be sure to!" the woman said.

He took their cups and led her back to his office. "You can't have lived in the UK and not get hooked on this stuff," he said. "Actually, a girl I liked got me hooked."

"Of course there's a woman involved," Sofia said drily.

"We were sixteen. She was still a girl, and I was a hound."

"Since we're on the topic of women—"

"I thought we were on the topic of tea. And taxes."

"Doesn't your ex work here?" she asked.

Sofia just now remembered the teary Brazilian beauty. She wondered if it was awkward for him having to see her every day. Would it be awkward if they ran into her now? He didn't answer until they were back on his couch.

"She's on the twenty-seventh floor and, as you know, I'm on the twenty-fifth."

"Are people on twenty-seven not allowed to fraternize with their colleagues on twenty-five?" she asked sweetly.

"Our paths don't cross very often," he said.

"That's a shame."

"It is," he said, serious. "I liked her."

He liked her, Sofia thought. How sweet.

"Things didn't end well," he said. "I was clumsy with it, but we had an *understanding*, or so I thought, anyway."

The Brazilian had thought they'd had a *connection*. An *amazing* connection.

"Try your tea," Jon said.

She eyed the mug with skepticism and took a small sip, then another. The warm rich liquid worked its way down her throat. "Not bad." She took another sip and got comfortable. "I like your office. It's calm."

Sofia doubted Jon had sacrificed anything by picking the lower floor. The view from his corner office was nothing short of spectacular.

"For all the time I spend here, it has to be."

"How long are your days?"

"Ten, twelve, fourteen hours, depending on what's going on."

Sofia was genuinely stunned. "That long? What happens when you have kids?"

"We're having kids?" he asked. "How many?"

She couldn't help but laugh. She laughed freely and happily for the first time in days. Only Jon could change her mood in the crummiest circumstances.

"I'm glad you two are having a good time."

Sofia looked up. Franco was in the doorway, looking sour and uncomfortable in the suit she'd insisted he wear to avoid looking like a common criminal. *Criminals are just people who've made bad choices.* She rested her mug on a side table. "We're just killing time."

He shot her a look that made her wonder if he'd expected them to sit around saying the Rosary until he got back.

"How did the meeting go?" Jon asked.

"Fine," Franco muttered. "She's going to get the ball rolling."

"That's encouraging," Sofia said.

"Yeah. I'll be heading out now."

Sofia nodded. "Okay."

Franco's cheeks lost color. "Bye. I guess."

"Have Alex validate your parking stub," Jon said.

Franco turned and exited the office, his back stiff. Sofia's first impulse was to ask him to stay and talk about his meeting. Jon's solid presence beside her stomped out that impulse.

"Do you need a ride back to work?" Jon asked.

His unshakable calm was so damn sexy.

"No. We drove in separately."

"Good. Finish your tea."

Sofia managed a smile. "I wish you'd taken his case."

She had a better understanding of how he'd earned his nickname: The Gun.

"Don't wish that," he said. "I'm not the lawyer for him."

"Why? Do you think he's guilty?"

"You know how the judicial system works, right?"

"Is that something they teach in law school?" she asked. "Talking down to people?"

"The man isn't *guilty* of anything. Not yet," Jon said. "Innocent until proven, and all that."

"He's innocent, Jon," Sofia said.

"How do you know?" Jon asked.

"I know him. He's not that clever."

"I won't dispute that."

Sofia urged him to be serious for a second. "People go to jail for tax evasion."

"People go to *prison* for tax fraud," Jon corrected her. "It's a felony in Florida. The laws here are among the toughest in the nation."

"Jail or prison, he won't survive a year."

How could she explain it? She'd wanted Franco out of her life, not incarcerated, and particularly for a crime he hadn't committed. She was convinced it was all a misunderstanding. A clever lawyer could make it go away.

"Sofia, you came to me for help. You've got to trust I won't let you down."

"But you didn't even take the case!" she cried.

"I'll stay on top of things."

Sofia reached into her purse for a business card and a pen. She jotted her cell phone number on the back of the card and handed it to him. "Will you keep me on top of things?"

Jon pocketed the card but turned her down. "I won't discuss him or his case with you. You're not the client. *He* is."

Sofia bit her lip, silenced. She must've looked worried because he asked, "Where's my Sofia?"

She understood the question. Where was the snappy woman he'd come to know and like? Here she was, dressed like a widow and fretting about her ex-fiancé. This was not a hot look under any standards.

"I'm here," she said. "Just burnt out."

She told him she was staying with her brother and not

sleeping well with the air mattress losing pressure at three in the morning and whatnot.

"If you need to get away, I can arrange that."

She indulged in the fantasy. What would it feel like to get away, to get lost with Jon? Hand in hand, hot sand under their feet and the sun on their backs. Dancing under the stars. Late night swims. How amazing would that be?

Sofia shot up to her feet, breathing hard and quick. "No, Jon. Thank you." She grabbed her purse, ready to leave. "You've done enough already."

What made her think Jon would take no for an answer?

The following week, Sofia stopped by Leila's agency for a work lunch. Their partnership was proving to be very lucrative and they had several projects queued up. The receptionist greeted her cheerily with a toss of her waist-length blond hair. "Ms. Silva, we're ordering juice from the bar downstairs. Will you have your usual spinach, apple and banana? Would you like to try adding kale this time? Or coconut water?"

"It's Sofia, and no kale or coconut."

"Very good," she said. "They're all in the conference room. Go right ahead."

"Thanks…" Sofia racked her memory and came up with her name. "Minnie."

"It's Minerva now."

"Why now?" Sofia asked.

She sat up straighter. "More professional, I think."

Sofia gave her a once-over. "Smart girl."

Leila's former agency was located in a small bungalow in Miami Beach and there was no conference room to speak of. This new location was an upgrade Sofia approved of. The conference room was large and spare. Its city views stood in contrast to the minimalist office decor. Leila and Brie were at the oval conference table.

"I was promised lunch," Sofia said. "Not kale juice."

"We're detoxing," Brie said.

Leila waived her in. "Come in. I've got news."

Sofia took a seat at the table and helped herself to a handful of jelly beans from a jar. "What's up?"

"It's about Jon Gunther," Brie said.

Sofia nearly choked on a jelly bean. "Oh?"

"Guess what he did," Brie said.

This week, Brie's naturally curly hair was dyed violet, matching her nails. Sofia glanced at her own nails. She could use a manicure. She could use a lot of things.

"I have no idea," Sofia said.

"Guess!" Brie insisted.

"I didn't come here for a guessing game, guys! Come out with it."

"Okay," Leila said. "Jon bought the house on Alton."

Sofia couldn't believe it. "I thought that house was under contract."

"That deal fell through." Leila leaned forward and whispered, "I shouldn't be telling you this—"

"So don't!"

Sofia and the others jumped at the sound of Nick's voice.

"Should we really be discussing our clients' business?" he asked.

"Sofia is practically a member of our team," Leila replied. "And she's been in on this deal from the start."

Nick picked up a laptop off the table. "Sofia, how's the Franco situation?"

"Under control," Sofia replied. She had no idea how Franco's case was progressing, but she was confident it was under control.

"Tell him I said 'good luck,'" Nick said, and walked out.

For a short while, they all sat chastised until Minerva called out, "All clear!"

Leila let out a sigh of relief and said, "He called two weeks ago Friday out of the blue and said he wanted the house *and* the furniture."

"I thought the furniture wasn't included," Sofia said reproachfully, as if it mattered now.

"It wasn't! It was all new pieces from Italy. I had to hustle hard for that."

Sofia felt heat rising to her face. Two weeks ago Friday, she and Jon had shared tiramisu and talked fondly about the house they figured had slipped through their fingers. Then, apparently, he'd turned around and bought it. Furniture and all.

Minerva entered with their drinks. Leila asked her to join them. While everyone sipped on their chilled beverages and commented on the miraculous benefits of kale and cayenne pepper, Sofia was swimming in a sea of mixed emotions.

"Back to Jon Gunther," Brie said.

Sofia agreed. She had a few questions. "Isn't that too much house for him?"

"It's a dope house," Brie said.

"Yeah," Minerva said. "It's hot."

"It's a solid investment," Leila said. "That's why I showed it to him before it hit the market. If he'd put in an offer straight away, he would've saved thousands."

"Three bedrooms?" Sofia said. "For just one person?"

"I see your point, but he won't be alone for long," Leila assured her. "Brie is ready to move in and set up a pole in the master suite."

Brie and Minerva exchanged a high-five. Sofia wasn't amused. Leila watched her closely, then she cleared the room.

"Back to work, you two," Leila said. "It's time for grown women talk."

Once alone, Leila sorted through a stack of files before her and handed Sofia an envelope. "This is for you."

Sofia eyed it suspiciously. "What's in there?"

"We closed on the house this morning. Jon is traveling to Atlanta tonight and he asked me to give this to you."

Sofia pressed the envelope between her hands and felt the shape of a key.

"He asked if I knew anyone who might be interested in house-sitting and I suggested you."

If you need to get away, I can arrange that.

The mastermind! He had Leila thinking the whole thing was her idea.

"He'll be gone for business, and he doesn't want it to sit empty," Leila said. "And you two seem to get along—"

"What do you mean by that?"

"Nothing," Leila said. She brought her straw to her lips to hide a mischievous smile.

"We don't get along any better than anyone else," Sofia said.

"Sure," Leila said. "But seeing that you're homeless now—"

"*Not* homeless!"

"Oh, please!" Leila protested. "Crashing at your brother's house can't be fun. You should get away. Take a staycation."

"What would I even do alone in that big house?" Sofia asked.

Leila sipped her kale, pineapple and ginger juice. "I can imagine a hundred things."

The conversation turned to work. They reviewed pending projects. Leila even went into detail about a listing on

Star Island the agency was coveting. Sofia didn't miss a beat. She urged Leila to rethink her concept of the open house. "At least for the more ambitious projects," Sofia said. "We're competing with multimillion-dollar developers. If we want to attract the top buyers, we have to give them an experience."

"Within a budget," Leila said.

"Obviously."

Leila went on about Star Island but, as far as Sofia was concerned, the meeting was over. She listened, sipping her juice, careful not to make any sudden moves. When Leila wasn't looking, she slipped the envelope in her purse. And when an appropriate amount of time had passed, she got up, mumbled something about traffic and left. Once in the garage, she rushed to her car and ripped the envelope open. The key fell onto her lap. There was a card with a security code and a cell phone number. A short note read: *The house is all yours. Get away.*

Chapter 12

At 11:30 p.m., Sofia received a text message. She'd hoped to get to sleep early, but a thunderstorm was making that impossible. The message itself assured she wouldn't get much sleep that night.

Boarding a plane to ATL. I left the gate unlocked. Make yourself at home.

The envelope with the key to Jon's new house was sitting on her nightstand. Sofia thought carefully before she typed an answer.

Sorry. Can't take you up on your offer.

His response came lightning-quick.

Can't or won't?

What did it matter?

Shouldn't.

But you're dying to.

Seriously? This man!

Is there room for your ego in the overhead compartment?

In first class? There'd better be.

Sofia rolled onto her belly and muffled a laugh in a pillow.

I'll be gone for a week. Enjoy my house.

She was halfway through typing Not gonna happen when a last message popped up.

Time to switch off electronics. Wish me a safe flight.

She sat up and looked around. Miguel's desk and work-out equipment had been pushed against a wall to make room for her. Here she was sleeping on an air mattress, her little fighter fish in a bowl on the floor, while she had in her possession the actual key to paradise. Without a second thought, she yanked back the bedsheets, walked over to the closet and pulled down a weekender bag. She threw clothes in from two dresser drawers and went into the bathroom to grab her toothbrush and toiletries. It was midnight when she drove out of the parking garage. The storm had passed. She didn't bother with the car's naviga-tion system. She knew the way.

It was about boxed wine, kettle-corn popcorn, and light meals picked up at Epicure Market. With very lim-ited wardrobe choices, she spent her days in a bikini and shorts. At night when it was cool, she slipped on a cotton sundress and switched on the outdoor fire pit. It was the spa retreat she needed and the personal time the magazines had mandated. It was the long-desired vacation that she'd kept putting off. For too long, work had been her single priority.

It had taken her about a day to slip into this groove. First, she had to get over feeling like a trespasser. It helped that the house was exactly as she remembered. Clean and furnished to her liking. A bit sterile, for sure. But when she flung her travel bag on the floor and kicked off her flip-flops, she'd made it her own. Then she had to get into vacation mode. When she called Ericka to leave her in charge, the younger woman was shocked but up for the challenge.

Sofia settled into a spacious guest room, having decided Jon's bed was off-limits. On her first night, however, she cuddled up with a blanket on the canopy bed out in the yard. Because the universe was kind, as Leila would say, she was blessed with infinite clear skies. She fell asleep under the stars and woke up at dawn, delighting in a sugar-pink sky.

Sofia was the work hard, play hard type of girl. *Play* was just another word for *network*. Rest had never factored into that equation until now. On her long daily walks to the gourmet market, she wondered if this was how most people spent their weekends, relaxing, enjoying their homes. *Enjoy my house.*

What was stopping her from enjoying Jon for a while? She wanted him for the same reasons some wanted to climb Mount Everest: the challenge and the thrill. He wasn't the type you took home to your mother. If you brought him around on Thanksgiving, by Christmas he'd likely be gone. How could she forget the sophisticated beauty he'd driven to tears? He'd led her to believe they had an amazing connection. And yet Sofia had forgotten about her. She had to dig deep to recall her teary face. All that mattered to her today was the promises Jon's eyes made. He'd be a delicious lover. He'd be fun. He'd be everything she needed in the moment. Wanting more would be greedy.

There'd be time enough to decide. In the meantime, Sofia threw a house party for one. It was her third night and she was feeling completely relaxed. She streamed music on her phone and opened a bottle of rosé. Her bathing suit was soggy and cold, and rather than slip it back on, she dove naked into the warm pool. This was living.

Jon charged out of Miami International Airport as if toxic gas had been pumped into the building. Without waiting for the crossing guard to give the okay, he bolted across multiple lanes of traffic toward the parking garage. Sofia was waiting. Thanks to the front door security cam to which he had remote access, he knew she was at the house. She'd been there for a couple of days and it was all he could do not to cancel his meetings and depositions and fly back to Miami.

Okay—she wasn't waiting for him. And he might've rounded up the number of days he'd expected to be away, by a lot. But she was so hard to resist, and made him act impulsively.

Her car was in the driveway. Jon couldn't describe the rush it gave him. He lost coordination, fumbling with his keys and struggling to get his suitcase through the door. Greeted by silence and partial darkness, he first noticed the fire in the backyard pit. He hesitated at the glass door, aware that he was invading someone's privacy. He ought to be more respectful. Maybe wait outside and call to give her a heads-up.

He ought to do that, but already he was out in the yard searching for her. She was in the pool. He caught a glimpse of her moving sultrily under the water, and hesitated again, feeling like an intruder in his own house.

Sofia suddenly broke the surface, letting out a cry. She smoothed her hair away from her face. "You!"

He approached the pool's edge. As the water swirled around her, he caught a glimpse of her nude breasts, honey brown with dark chocolate nipples. His brain slowed, laboring to process this information. Sofia was naked…in his pool.

Their eyes met and the negotiations began. How were they going to play this? Should he be a gentleman and walk away? Offer her a towel? Should he wait for her cue? Chin raised and eyes focused, she didn't seem shy. Her breath had steadied. She wasn't even blushing.

Jon felt like he was under her spell.

"If I'd known this house came with a naked woman in the pool," he said, "I'd have bought it on the spot."

She didn't laugh. She kept her eyes on him, and he could just hear the old wheels grinding. She was making up her mind about him. He stayed quiet, not wanting to tip the scale in one way or the other. This was her decision to make. He'd do whatever she asked.

She asked for nothing. Jon watched, fascinated, as she swam over to the ladder and climbed out, silver water pouring off the slope of her back. She came to stand before him, her skin baked to rich terra cotta by the sun. He could've fallen to his knees. He could've died right there. Sofia… finally…of all the times their paths had crossed, she'd worn so many protective masks and he'd never had a glimpse of *this* woman.

"Hello, stranger," he said.

She grabbed his tie with her damp hands and deftly loosened the knot. "Do you always travel dressed like this?"

"I left for the airport straight from a meeting."

"Poor you."

"Did you have a nice day, dear?" he asked.

The tie fell silently to the slate tile. "You know what? We've talked enough, you and I."

She'd get no argument from him.

She stripped him of the jacket and the shirt underneath, all the while laying down the law. "This is a temporary thing. Okay?"

"More than okay," he replied.

It wasn't remotely okay, but Jon knew better than to show his hand. Besides, he had mastered this game. She had no idea who she was up against. She didn't want to talk? No problem. He gripped her by her slippery waist, lifted her off the ground and tossed her into the pool. She landed with a splash. He undressed and dove in after her. In no time, he had her cornered. The water was cool but the heat between them was rising.

She rested her palms on his chest and brushed her lips against his. Jon took his time with their first kiss. He wanted her to know what she'd been missing—and for what? She whimpered under his kiss. He growled when she wrapped her legs around his waist and rubbed her soft nakedness against his body. They broke the kiss and went back at it harder. Stealing a second to gasp for air, she whispered his name. He reminded her of the rules. "No talking."

He pulled her under water and there he cupped her breasts and teased the nipples with his teeth. He would've gone at it forever if his lungs weren't on fire. He had to get her out of the pool and onto a bed. Conveniently enough, there was a bed located only steps away.

Stretched out on the canopy bed, they managed to say a lot without words. Let me see you. Touch me. Grip here. Wrap your fingers. Tighter. He left her only to get a condom in his wallet. She was holding on to the bedposts when he got back. Ready for him. Jon kneeled between the V of her legs, and she closed her eyes. He waited patiently until she opened them again, looking at him questioningly through lowered lashes.

He shook his head, no. She didn't get to hide.

When he had her attention, he ran a finger along the opening between her legs. She arched her back. Breaking the rules, she murmured, "Jon, please."

But words weren't necessary. There was nothing he couldn't read in her eyes. They were *pleading* with him.

Jon climbed over her, kissed her full on the mouth, then brushed his fingertip over her lips so she could taste her own arousal. He had wanted to bring her to this point since the day they'd met—the point of shameless begging. He wasn't going to waste the moment. He ran his palms along the wet skin of her thighs, coaxing a moan from her parted lips.

"I got you, Sofia."

Her eyes narrowed, telling him she'd caught the nuanced meaning of his words. *I got you.* He eased himself inside her. Her fingers tightened around his arms and she let out a cry. Jon held it all in. He didn't move. She was hot and tight around him, and he could not move. Then she rolled her hips back and he was underwater again, sinking, fighting to break the surface.

Chapter 13

Everything hurt in a tender way. Cradled in Jon's arms, Sofia knew where they were. How and when they'd moved from the backyard to the master suite was a mystery. She lifted the comforter and scooted out of bed. She looked around for her clothes, then realized that she hadn't been wearing any. This was going to be the walk of shame to top them all, even if only a few steps down a hallway. On tiptoe, she rounded the bed, bumped a knee against the dresser and blindly searched for the doorknob.

"The bathroom is the other door," Jon said, his voice groggy.

"I know." She found the doorknob and opened the door slightly, letting in a triangle of light. "My stuff is in the other room."

Jon rolled onto his back and stretched. "Your stuff will be there in the morning."

That was a good point. And yet she clung to the door-knob. This was how things got complicated. You stayed a night or two and never wanted to leave. That was the opposite of fun.

"Sofia, don't go."

She loved the way he said her name, drawing it out, leaning heavily on the *f* and making it his own.

"Come on." He lifted the comforter, inviting her back into the cocoon.

What could she do? She was feeling groggy herself. The

open door had let in a draft. She was naked and cold. Her legs were stiff with fatigue. How could she make it down the hall to her room? It would take only two steps to make it back to him.

She released the door handle and dove back into bed. He kissed the back of her neck, the rough stubble of his cheek chaffing her skin. "Tomorrow, bring your stuff in this room, and I'll bring mine."

She closed her eyes and told herself she was too tired to argue. They could talk about it in the morning.

In the morning, Jon was half-naked at the foot of the bed. Freshly showered and shaved, brown skin like toffee, a white dress shirt left open over boxer shorts. Eyebrows drawn, he was scrolling his phone. Sofia couldn't fight back a smile. Could she wake up to this view every morning?

"You got a head start," she said. "That's not fair."

He looked up from his task and gazed at her for a long moment. Then he tossed the phone onto the nightstand and climbed on top of her, light and quick. He caught her chin between his teeth. When she turned away, he went after her ear, pushing her hair out of the way. Sofia squirmed as her whole body awakened to pleasure.

"Aren't you going to be late for whatever you're dressing for?" she asked.

He trailed kisses down her neck and asked what her plans were for the day.

"Now that you're back, my staycation is over," she said. "I'll be checking out of Hotel Gunther today."

Jon rolled onto his side, relieving her of his weight. Immediately, though, she missed it.

"That wasn't what we agreed to," he said. "You're moving your stuff in here."

"Did I agree to that?" she asked.

"Silence is acquiescence," he said.

Sofia hated to admit it, but she loved the sexy lawyer talk.

Jon reached over her, grabbed his phone off the bedside table and called his office. "I won't be in today or tomorrow. See you Monday."

He hung up and tossed the phone across the bed, out of reach. "Now," he said, those brown eyes bright with mischief, "we can staycation here or get out of here, go to the beach or down to the Keys. You decide."

He nuzzled her neck and said he'd like to lick salt off her skin. The decision had been made.

He asked for a couple of hours to get organized and headed out with a shopping list. Sofia kept busy with laundry, dumping her bathing suit, sundresses, T-shirts and cutoffs into the washing machine. She showered and shaved and folded her dry clothes into her weekender bag. Anything to avoid the question: am I really going away to Key West with this man? The YES hiding in the tall grass of her mind would scare the daylights out of her, so she avoided it.

He returned with a gym bag stuffed with clothes and supplies, courtesy of CVS: sunblock, mosquito repellant and a large box of condoms.

She pulled the box out of the thin plastic bag. "Any chance we're going to spend time getting to know each other on this trip?"

"That's all we're going to do." He opened the refrigerator door and frowned at its poor contents. He pulled out her last box of wine and tossed it in the trash. "Let's start now."

"Oh?" Sofia hopped onto the kitchen counter and swung her bare legs.

"Why did you and Franco break up?"

Sofia coughed, her throat tight. "Excuse me?"

"I understand there was a breakup and a cover-up," he said, still engrossed with the refrigerator. "But I don't know why you two lovebirds broke up in the first place."

Lovebirds? "Why are we talking about this?"

"I want to know the full story. Otherwise, it'll drive me nuts."

"There's nothing to tell." Sofia hopped off the counter. "It's the same lame story. You fall in love. You fall out of love. Case closed, counselor."

He shut the refrigerator door and studied her, his expression inscrutable.

"We really should get going," Sofia said. "Traffic is going to build up."

Speeding along the Seven Mile Bridge, Sofia felt uneasy. The strip of concrete stretched over the channel where the ocean and the bay mingled. No matter how many times she'd made this trip, it left her unsettled. With the top of the convertible down, she felt weightless and unanchored. She worried she might fly away.

"You okay?" Jon asked.

They hadn't spoken much, but that was his fault. Why would he bring up Franco after their first night together? Why would he question her about her past while she was holding a box of condoms? It was rude and tactless, to say nothing else.

A motorcycle sped past them, recklessly close.

"Keep your eyes on the road," she said.

He kept his left hand on the wheel of the Porsche and reached for her with the right, linking his fingers with hers. "Don't worry."

Sofia closed her eyes. They were speeding away from their city and their exes, and she hoped they could leave it all behind. It was as scary and exciting as crossing a bridge, and yet they made it across.

"We're booked."

"That's right," Sofia said to the front desk clerk. "I booked your last available room online." They were hungry, hot and worn-out from the trip. Sofia knew a great place for conch fritters but they first had to settle the small matter of lodging. "I have a confirmation number and everything."

Desperate, Sofia searched for the confirmation email on her phone. The bed-and-breakfast had appealed to them straight away. Its gingerbread style with a sloped roof and shuttered windows was charming. Located on the south end of Duval Street, it was a short walk to the beach.

The clerk shook her head. "That might've been a computer glitch."

"Not one single vacancy?" Jon asked.

The clerk was in the throes of an allergy attack. She dabbed her watery eyes with a tissue. "There's one, but—"

"We'll take it." Jon reached for his wallet.

"Wait one minute," she said. "It's a long-term stay suite. It comes with a kitchenette and a private balcony."

Sofia put away her phone. "Nothing wrong with that."

"Long-term stay," the clerk repeated, more slowly this time. "We don't book it for less than one week, seven nights."

It was Thursday, and they planned to return to Miami on Sunday afternoon. They had three wondrous nights ahead of them—if they could book a room.

"We'll book it for seven, stay for three," Jon said. "Any objections?"

The clerk blew her nose. "All I need is a credit card."

Jon slid a platinum card across the desk.

"I'll throw in one night free," the clerk said cheerily. Then she sneezed up a storm.

With keys in hand, they followed a porter across a courtyard to the stairs leading to their second-floor suite. Jon stepped aside at the landing so that Sofia could go ahead. Sofia turned to face him and touched his arm. "We'll split the bill."

He took her hand off his arm and rested it on the iron stair rail. "We'll talk about it later."

By "later," she guessed he meant never. So after lunch, while they were hanging out at the hotel courtyard for beer and live music, Sofia slipped away to the front desk to settle their bill. A new clerk, bright-eyed and allergy-free, pulled up their account.

"Suite 210? There's no balance."

"Are you sure?" Sofia asked. "We were supposed to pay the balance at checkout."

The clerk reviewed the account once again. "No balance, as of one thirty-five this afternoon. You're still responsible for any in-room entertainment and mini-bar products you enjoy during your stay. You're welcome to settle those fees at checkout."

Sofia drummed the counter with her fingertips. At one thirty-five they'd been at lunch, chomping on conch fritters. When had the sneaky bastard found the time?

Jon was at a table under the shade of an almond tree. A longneck beer bottle was waiting for her. She confronted him, hands on hips.

"I know what you did."

He grinned, flashing a row of straight white teeth. "Then I know what you tried to do."

"I can afford to pay my way, you know," she said. "I can't have you paying for everything."

"Does that mean you don't want this beer?"

"Jon…"

"This trip was my idea and my treat. Plain. Simple."

The band started playing "Margaritaville," as likely mandated by Key West local laws. Sofia took a sip from the bottle and willed herself to calm down. There was nothing she could do about the hotel tab without coming off as petty. While she mulled this over, he rested his Heineken bottle on the table, drew her onto his lap and threaded his cold hand through the slit of her dress. She relaxed against him, sang along with the band and tried to put the whole business out of her mind. They hadn't come all this way to argue. Still, she had one last question.

She wrapped an arm around his neck. "Just out of curiosity, when did you settle the account? We were never apart."

"Since when are you this interested in transparency?"

"What does that mean?" she asked.

"You have your secrets. I have mine."

She didn't get what he was alluding to, but the set of his eyes tipped her off. She jerked upright, nearly toppling backward. "This can't be about this morning. Are you serious?"

"Dead serious."

Sofia jumped off his lap and headed for the stairs. She locked herself in their suite's bathroom and turned on the shower. Her anger was reaching its boiling point, and she wondered while undressing how much it would cost to Uber back to Miami.

She understood new couples usually had a "talk" about their exes, but this was taking things too far. First of all, they weren't a couple. Second of all…he could go to hell.

Jon knocked on the door. "Sofia, I'm sorry. Are you crying?"

Crying! Was he kidding? Sofia wrapped a towel around

her bare breasts and swung open the bathroom door to confront him, dry-eyed.

"Jon, I don't have the words to describe how big of a *jerk* you're being right now!"

He didn't back down. "I've answered all your questions about Viv. I told you the truth even when the answers didn't exactly make me look good."

Viv? Is that what he called her? Was that short for something sultry like Viviana? "I want to know what you're hiding," Jon said.

"I'm not hiding anything," Sofia retorted. "I didn't like the way you sprang the question on me, that's all."

"Granted," he said. "I was bullish with it, but it's eating me."

"Why? What does it matter?"

"I hate that you're so protective of him."

A tap on the bedroom door put an end to round one. A woman called out, "Housekeeping!"

Jon went to the door. "Come back later. My girl is getting dressed."

As far as Sofia was concerned, those words…*my girl*… put an end to the whole fight. But he didn't have to know that.

The Key West sunset was a natural attraction and, over lunch, they'd planned to watch it along with every other tourist on the island at Mallory Square. But what was meant to be a romantic excursion had turned sour. The walk to the square took longer than it should have. They dragged their feet, burdened by the silence between them. Bicycle taxis whizzed past them. They arrived just in time to the waterfront plaza. Every single juggler, fire-eater and accordionist in the Lower Keys had showed up to entertain the masses. Sofia shivered when Jon placed a hand on the small of her back, guiding her toward the seawall for a better view of the one spectacle that was absolutely free. Cell-phone cameras snapped all around them in a collective effort to capture the ephemeral beauty of the moment: the sun sinking into the Gulf of Mexico in sheer washes of orange and pink, leaving behind a deep lavender sky. Sofia turned around and buried her face in Jon's chest. She couldn't shoulder the weight of their silence anymore. If she had to cave, she'd cave.

She gripped his T-shirt and mumbled, "He sexted women when he was bored."

He gently pried her away. "What?"

Sofia couldn't look him in the eye. Jon had been wrong about her trying to protect Franco. She'd been trying to protect herself from the embarrassment of having to tell her new lover that her old lover hadn't found her that interesting and made up for what she was lacking with apps, screenshots and emojis.

"He met women online and was chatting, sexting, you name it. One night I caught him—"

"Okay. I got it."

"I *want* to tell you everything, Jon. It's not easy."

"I'm sorry I harassed you," he said. "Sorry he put you through that. Sorry for all of it."

"I'm here with you because I want you," she said. "Can't we leave the past behind?"

Her hair was flapping every which way in the breeze. He gathered fistfuls and pulled her into a kiss. They kissed in front of their fellow tourists and the vendors that catered to them. They kissed long and slow in front of couples, kids, contortionists and cartoonists. Sofia thought she might lose her head, but it was her heart that escaped her, drifting unnoticed out to sea.

Chapter 14

Sofia in the sun was a gift. Her skin glowed. She wore her hair wet, slicked back and curling at the tips. At the beach she was a playful child, jumping onto Jon's back as they waded into the water. She spent an hour building igloos in the sand. They'd rented two lounge chairs, but used only one. The other held all her *stuff*—a beach day survival kit that she hardly touched. Now, she rested her head on his chest while he stroked her back. The smell of salt on her skin combined with the lazy back and forth of the surf was giving him ideas.

A woman with shaggy blond hair approached them, asking in a French-Canadian accent whether this was the beach where Diana Nyad had come to shore. At sixty-four, Nyad had swum the straights from Cuba to Key West, risking death by dehydration or shark attack.

Sofia was quick to confirm it. "Yup! This is where she made history."

"She's one of my heroes," the woman said. "I have no intention of swimming with the sharks when I retire, but you see what I mean."

Sofia agreed. "I'll swim laps in my pool."

Jon scanned the shoreline. The ordinary beach, now apparently a historic landmark, didn't rank as a wonder of the world. He was convinced the sand had been brought in by the truckload. The ocean rushed forward in thin pale sheets onto a rug of brown, mangled seaweed. And it smelled of sulfur. Beyond the beach, the breadth of the ocean was awe-inspiring. And he had to admit, when sunlight touched the surface, the metallic glow was gorgeous.

Not as gorgeous as Sofia.

"Are you two on your honeymoon?" the woman asked.

"Who? Us?" Sofia asked, stunned.

"You two can't keep your hands off each other. It's lovely to see. But I shouldn't assume. This is Key West, after all."

Why was Sofia so shocked? Jon knew she thought their days were numbered and that was fine for now, but why did he feel she knew the exact number?

The woman returned to a frayed towel stretched out on the sand. Jon waited before asking why she was surprised that strangers thought they were together.

She twisted to face him, sitting on her knees. "Being together and being married is not the same thing, Jon."

He tilted his head, looking past her. "You've only got to look at them to know that's true."

She glanced over her shoulder, spotting the couple rounding up kids and dutifully packing up toys. "What's wrong with them?"

"What's wrong with *us*, Sofia?" he asked. "Why do I feel it's over before it's started?"

"Because I'm not deluded, Jon," she replied. "I know you think marriage is for suckers like them."

She pointed to their reference couple now negotiating a peace agreement with a screaming toddler.

"I never said that," he replied.

"Okay," she said. "Tell me one time you met someone, fell in love and had a vision of forever."

"Define 'forever.'"

"Jon, I'm serious."

And so was he, he realized. This was not the time or place for this conversation. But if she was going to bring it up…

"I'm capable of making a commitment," he said. "If that's what you're asking."

"Name a time you actually did commit," she persisted.

"Law school. She was L3. I was L1."

"Is that like a sergeant dating a soldier?" she teased.

"Do you want to hear this or not?" he asked.

By the set of her jaw, he knew she didn't want to hear it, just like she didn't want to see the rain clouds gathering over the horizon.

"Skip to the relevant part," she said. "We *all* know you have a thing for lawyers."

"How do we *all* know that?" he asked. "Was there a press conference I missed?"

"Your *Viv* was a lawyer."

"My what?" Jon laughed and laughed. It wasn't possible to add any more contempt to one syllable than she had with that name.

"Sofia… I know you're not jealous. Right?"

She drummed his chest with her delicate fists. "Don't laugh at me!"

At that moment, three women in color-coordinated bathing suits stepped up to the lounge chair they shared. He hadn't seen them coming. Now that they were standing there, casting a long shadow, he wanted to shoo them away. Whoever they were, their timing couldn't have been worse.

"You guys!" Sofia cried. Her voice had an uphill curve.

One of the three stepped forward as the leader. "Surprised to see us? You wouldn't be if you'd answered any one of our fifty or so emails."

Sofia scooted off the chaise. "Our B and B has no Wi-Fi."

Jon shifted. Where was his sharp-tongued Sofia, the woman who'd been arguing with him every leg of this very short trip?

"Wi-Fi?" the leader repeated, incredulous. She was thin,

with brittle limbs and long brown hair. "We've been trying to reach you to schedule this trip for *weeks*. Plus, I asked you about it at your parents' anniversary party—"

"That party is a blur," Sofia said. "Mom drove me crazy. I'm here to recover from it."

"We see that."

The three women looked pointedly at Sofia, then Jon, then Sofia again. Sofia looked as if she were melting under the heat of their combined stares. Her cheeks took on a hue that for all they'd been through, he'd never seen.

She seemed helpless.

Jon could do her the favor of slinking away but he was not that man, the meek elephant in the room. So instead, he rolled up to his feet and unfolded to his full stature, and looked down at the four women. They didn't get to talk around him. And Sofia would have to learn someday that she didn't get to speak for him.

"Hi, everyone," he said. "I'm Jon."

All eyes were on him. Sofia touched his arm and said, "Jon, this is my cousin Merci… I mean Mercedes, and our friends Sheryl and Riya."

The three women curtly said hello.

"What's everyone drinking?" Jon asked.

That simple question switched the dynamics.

"Strawberry daiquiri!"

"Piña colada!"

"Margarita, no salt!"

Sofia looked up at him, her eyes brimming with gratitude. "Nothing for me. Thanks."

Everything for you.

Jon's heart was pounding at the thought. He didn't want to leave her, but felt it was best to give her space. He told her that he'd be at the bar. "I'll have a waiter send over your drinks."

* * *

Merci and the others were the last people Sofia had expected to see. It was as if her past had come to snatch her out of this new world she was exploring on her own terms. She had come very close to surrendering to their authority. One more pointed glare from Merci and she'd have stuck out her wrists, resigned, ready to be cuffed and hauled away. But then Jon had stood beside her and she'd recovered fully. Sofia watched Jon walk away while Merci, Riya and Sheryl piled onto the chaise with all her stuff. He was showing extraordinary restraint, considering that he'd been cast out of his own beach chair by what looked like three former members of Destiny's Child.

Reluctantly, Sofia sat opposite them, facing the firing squad.

Merci attacked first. "You're cheating on Franco?"

"No, no, no, no, no!" Sofia couldn't let *that* be the takeaway from all this.

"That's what it looks like," Merci said.

"Franco and I are done," Sofia said. That was all she would say. If Jon had to pry the truth out of her like a pearl from a clam, she certainly wasn't going to give it up to these three.

"And when were you planning on telling us?" Merci asked.

"Soon," Sofia replied. "Look, we haven't even told our parents."

Riya leaned forward and asked, "Is it because of his legal troubles?"

So the news had gotten out. Sofia hesitated, not wanting to confirm any wild rumors they might have heard. "No. That's not it at all."

Riya tossed her a doubtful look.

"We know all about it," Sheryl said. "Something about taxes."

Now that she thought about it, "something about taxes" sounded way better than "something about sexting." At the end of the day, Franco's legal problems were a matter of public record. But what he chose to do with his smartphone data plan was his own damn business.

"It didn't take you long to move on," Merci said drily.

Sofia noted how sure her friends were that she'd dumped Franco.

The waiter arrived with a tray of cocktails, including a Tequila Sunrise for Sofia. She reached for it with a shaky hand. Jon knew she didn't mess around with fruity drinks. Had he ordered the bona fide vacation cocktail so she could fit in with her friends? She tipped her glass. The orange and red swirl took her back to their sunset kiss.

"So, who the hell is *he*?" Merci resumed the attack.

"Jon, you mean?" Sofia said. "He's a lawyer, a good one. New Jersey native."

"This can't be happening," Sheryl said. "You and Franco have been together for so long."

"Too long," Sofia said.

The three stared at her, disappointment molding their features. Sofia felt sickened, as if she'd told a four-year-old that the mall Santa was also the mall-parking attendant on the off-season. She lowered her eyes, sipped her cocktail, brushed sand off her knees and prayed the inquisition would be over soon. When she glanced up again, her friends were still staring at her.

"Look," Sofia said wearily. "I kept things quiet for my mom's sake—that's it. And I get it. You're team Franco, but—"

"This is life," Riya said. "There are no teams. We're just asking."

"I'm not team anyone," Sheryl said. "Except maybe this new guy. I'm into him."

"My piña is delicious," Riya said. "Thank him, please."

Sofia studied her friends with gradual understanding. They'd met Jon for all of five minutes, but that was enough. He'd won them over. Merci was the only holdout.

"I was your maid of honor!" Merci cried. "And you didn't tell me?"

Sofia's attitude softened. Merci had been so looking forward to the wedding. As a little girl, she'd married off all her dolls in frilly dollar-store dresses. She was single, waiting for the elusive Mr. Right and believed in happy endings. That did not include a canceled wedding and a bride moving on with a lawyer from New Jersey.

"Merci, I'm sorry," Sofia said. "You're right. I should've told you."

"Yes, you should've," Merci snapped.

"How about we meet up later?" Riya proposed. "We've got reservations at La Te Da. Join us!"

"No," Sofia said. "Jon and I have dinner plans."

Riya frowned. She was a nurse, and her inclination was always to heal and restore. Sofia appreciated the effort, but she had to shut her down. She did not want to meet with them at La Te Da or anywhere else. All she wanted was to resume her vacation still in progress.

"We're not at the meet-the-friends stage yet," Sofia said.

And she doubted they'd ever get to that stage. Still, Sheryl's next comment didn't sit well with her.

"He's clearly the rebound guy," Sheryl said. "Can I have him when you cut him loose?"

"Okay." Sofia stood up. "We're done here."

She doled out hugs and kisses like lollipops at a pediatrician's office and said goodbye. She joined Jon at the bar and placed her empty glass before him.

"Thanks for this," she said. "I needed it."

"Do we get them to sign non-disclosure agreements?" he asked. "I could draft one on a cocktail napkin."

"That won't be necessary, smart-ass."

She reached for his hand and gave his long brown fingers a squeeze. Throughout the day, no matter what they'd been discussing, no matter how thorny those discussions got, they'd managed to stay physically connected. She wanted to reestablish that.

"You panicked back there," he said.

"People who knew me and Franco as this stable couple may have a hard time accepting me and anyone else," she said.

"Will you ever accept it?" he asked.

Sofia slid off her bar stool and went to him. Clearly, holding hands wasn't going to do the trick. She slipped her arms around his waist and kissed his warm neck.

"You know they're still watching," he said.

"In that case…"

Sofia kissed him full on the mouth and hoped he tasted orange and grenadine on her tongue. After all, this was their vacation.

Chapter 15

The extended-stay suite had a kitchenette with a window overlooking the courtyard. Banana trees hung limp, their leaves more yellow than green and heavy with the night's rain. Beyond the hotel walls, the neighborhood was waking to the relentless crowing of large red roosters. For Sofia, it was like waking up in La Vega, the town in the Dominican Republic that her father was from and where she and Miguel had spent their summers growing up.

Today, they'd be heading home. Sofia breathed in the fresh salt air and realized that life in the Keys was very much what people imagined life in Miami to be. Miami had its welcoming outer shell, consisting of tropical weather and a party vibe. Its core, though, was tough and inhospitable. Jon had lived all over the world, but Sofia couldn't imagine living anywhere else. For all its flaws, Miami was home. Jon could pack up and leave at any time. True, he'd bought a house. But what were houses if not investments? Hadn't Leila made that clear? The house was an asset. Something he could sell, bank the money and move on.

Sofia pushed those thoughts out of her mind. She filled a moka pot with water, spooned ground coffee into the basket and placed it on the electric burner. The closest she ever came to meditation was when standing watch over her Nespresso machine. This simple stainless steel pot was primitive compared to her top-of-the-line coffeemaker, and waiting in quiet anticipation for it to boil over with fresh brewed coffee was a nice change.

She heard Jon stumble around in the bedroom. Last night, their last in Key West, they'd had dinner at a restaurant overlooking the water. They'd discussed politics over a world-class seafood meal. Then they taxied over to Better Than Sex where they shared a decadent dessert and licked unctuous chocolate off the backs of their spoons and talked about global warming. They ended the evening with a nightcap at The Rum Bar and walked back to the hotel at two in the morning. Hand in hand, they strolled past strings of A-frame houses painted Easter egg colors. Sofia had rolled onto their bedroom floor, doubling over with laughter at a story the bartender had told them. She flopped onto her back, the hem of her skirt fanning out over the wood floor. Jon stretched out next to her and the look in his eyes, a most adoring look, had sobered her up in a flash.

"It's our last night," she'd said.

At last, it was time to talk about the one topic they'd avoided all evening.

"Our last night *here*," he said.

She shook her head from side to side. "I like it here. I don't want to go back."

He crawled over her, trapped her hips between his knees. "We can fake our own deaths and stay here forever, like the bartender's girlfriend."

Sofia burst into laughter again. "Wasn't that the craziest thing?"

"Is there anything you want on our last night?" he asked.

Emboldened by the free spirit of Key West, Sofia had reached between his legs and grabbed what she wanted. She looked down at her hands now, checking if they were changed somehow.

* * *

Jon came into the kitchen wearing nothing but boxer shorts. Sofia wasn't wearing anything at all.

He kissed her shoulder. "Coffee smells good."

A good coffee bean released the scent of the earth that nurtured it. The aroma rising from the little pot was certainly rich, but Sofia wanted to smell his skin. She turned to face him and was greeted by an impressive erection stretching through soft cotton boxers.

She looked up to the wicked brown eyes. "Excuse me. What do you plan to do with that?"

"Up to you," he said.

She smiled. "I have an idea."

Sofia sank to her knees and tugged at the waist of his shorts. She felt his hand dive into her messy hair and tighten its grip.

"Sofia, I'm keeping you," he whispered.

She glanced up at him, shocked by the determination in his voice. She wasn't a thing that could be kept, but she was willing to give him a pass. He was sleep-deprived, and all statements made before coffee were ridiculous.

She took him in her mouth.

The coffee percolated and spilled over.

They'd delayed their departure until the last possible minute and it was dark by the time they made it back to Miami. Jon was humming to himself when they pulled up to the house. Sofia was biting her nails. She had a simple exit plan and ran through it point by point. As soon as Jon parked, she'd grab her bag out of the trunk and make a mad dash to her own car still in the driveway. She had no choice but to make a clean break of it. If she stepped foot in that house, even just to pee, she wouldn't leave.

Jon opened the garage by remote control and was glad to see the space crammed with boxes. "Yes!"

"What happened here?" Sofia asked.

"I'm officially moved in. I paid some guys to do this while we were gone."

"Can those same guys help me?"

"Move your stuff here?" he asked. In the dark, his grin flashed white. "I can arrange it."

Sofia made an effort to laugh at the joke. "Actually, Jon, I think it's time—"

He got out of the car before she finished her sentence and went straight to the trunk. He had both their bags by the time she caught up with him.

"I'll take mine. Thanks."

"This?" He lifted her stuffed weekender as if it weighed nothing. "I got it."

She looked past him at the house; its geometric facade was intriguing and inviting. She knew all too well every convenience and comfort it had to offer.

"I'm hungry," he said. "That drive gave me an appetite. What should we order?"

He spoke casually, as if they weren't in the middle of a power struggle, which they absolutely were. Sofia's stomach betrayed her, growling a response. The last thing she wanted was to drive back to Miguel's place and have to scavenger for food on her own.

Plus, she had to pee.

In the morning, she told herself. *You can leave in the morning.*

"How about pizza?" he asked, looking very cool.

"Pizza is good."

She walked past him, heading up the driveway to the front door. She hadn't conceded a thing, she reasoned. She'd come to this decision on her own. Still, the gleam of amusement in Jon's eyes when he joined her on the front steps annoyed her. Desperate for the last word, she said, "Don't forget to close the garage door."

They took the pizza out to the yard. It felt good to be back, Sofia had to admit. It felt too good. She turned to Jon seated beside her on a low teak bench facing the pool. "Jon?"

He nodded, taking a healthy bite out of a slice of pepperoni pizza. Her slice was half eaten on her paper plate. Her stomach was in knots.

"In the morning—"

"Sofia," he mumbled, his mouth full. "Isn't this good pizza?"

Oh, God. How adorable was he?

She dabbed at the corners of his mouth with a napkin. "It's the best."

In the morning, Sofia brushed her teeth while Jon ran the shower. She watched him undress in the bathroom mirror, really just stepping out of a pair of shorts and kicking it to the side. Her heart lurched forward. When he gestured for her to join him, she yanked off her T-shirt without a moment's pause. Water blasted out of six showerheads, massaging her aching muscles. Jon squeezed the last of her shower gel into his rough palm and lathered her body. He was working the suds down her legs when she felt the imperative to speak up again.

"Jon, after work," she said, "I'll be heading straight—"

Jon reached for a bar of soap and rubbed it between her legs. Desire shot through her, forcing her head back. Her hair got caught in the shower stream. With warm water pouring over her and Jon's strong fingers inside her, she came close to orgasm. But then he abruptly cut off the water, wrapped her in a towel and carried her into the bedroom.

On the bed, she tossed aside the towel and moved quickly to sit astride him.

"Hold it."

He reached for the last of the condoms on the bedside table. She worked to make his task impossible. Her eager hands explored him everywhere. She stroked the wide plane of his back, enjoying the play of his muscles. When she moved in for a kiss, he pulled away.

"What have you been trying so hard to tell me?" he asked.

Sofia froze. Her timing had been off all along, but now *really* wasn't the time to get into it.

He brushed her hair away from her face. "You want to leave me? Is that it?"

She softened in his arms. "I don't *want* to. But I think it's time."

He kissed her neck. By now, he'd figured out all her tender spots. "If you don't want to, and I don't want you to, what's there to think about?"

"I can't stay here."

"We don't have to tell anybody," he said. "I can keep your secrets, too."

That sounded like a plan that she could get behind. Maybe. She wasn't sure. She'd have to think about it. Although, what he called secrecy, she called discretion. But they could debate that later. For the moment, she had more pressing concerns. She traced his lips with her fingers, asking again for that kiss. He drew her to him and kissed her like no man had ever kissed her. He made love to her with that same masterful assurance.

Was there really anything to think about?

Chapter 16

"Lay it on me," Jon said to Stephanie. "How much trouble is Ramirez in?"

As soon as Jon returned to work, he'd made a beeline to Stephanie Conwell's office. His number one focus, taking priority over his own caseload, was to clear Sofia's ex's name. He had no intention of sitting idly by while that bastard drained Sofia, taking advantage of her misguided sense of loyalty. And, as a matter of pride, he could not lose this case. He'd promised Sofia he'd stay on top of things, which really meant he'd handle it.

"The state alleges sales taxes were collected on used cars, but not remitted, right? It's not clear that Mr. Ramirez had any knowledge of this. Our client was in charge of the new car division, mostly leases. Not much wiggle room there. However, two businesses operated under the same umbrella. There is a used car division. I'm still looking into it. So far he's complied with all my requests and has been very cooperative."

Jon stood to leave. "Let me know if there are any developments."

"Of course," Stephanie said. "On another note, how did your vacation go?"

"A man takes two days off and it's news," Jon said.

"In this place, yes," she said. "But you look so rested and happy. It makes me want to get away."

"Not before you clear Ramirez of all charges. Then I'll pay for your vacation myself."

Jon whistled as he took the stairs down to his floor. He owed his happiness to Sofia. And now, keeping her close and protected was his goal. Without saying too much, they'd reached an agreement this morning. He wanted her to stay. She wanted to stay. But it was a temporary solution. So long as her past held her back, they couldn't move forward.

Back at his desk, Jon thumbed through his calendar but his thoughts remained with Sofia. If she let him, he'd be the man Franco had not been. He'd clear up the messes of her past and give her the future she deserved. If she let him.

"Welcome to Star Island!" Leila cried. "I'm your host."

Two days later, Sofia was back in her element, in pencil skirts and peep-toe pumps. Leila was serving her real-estate gold on a platter: twenty-thousand square feet of waterfront paradise on an exclusive island off Miami Beach.

"What do you think?" Leila asked.

"I'm speechless," Sofia replied.

In fact, she was thinking Jon was going to *die* when she told him about this house later tonight. It had all his favorite toys: a bay front *and* a rooftop pool, a garage big enough to hold six cars, a master suite with sunset views.

Leila walked over to what at first glance appeared to be a framed glass wall. "These doors retract," she said. "And when they do…boom!" She opened her arms wide to encompass the city skyline and cruise ships in the distance.

Sofia slipped off her sunglasses and eyed the empty room more critically—retracting doors and all. Promoting this property would be a huge project. It was bound to cement her reputation as a top Miami player. Whatever

Leila and Nick were expecting from her, she had to exceed it. This wasn't the time to cash in friendship bonus chips.

"Can you imagine living here?" Leila asked.

It was a question Leila asked often. Can you imagine it? Living in this colossal home? No, Sofia couldn't imagine it. She preferred her present address, albeit only temporary. It was far cozier, for one thing. This felt like a hollowed-out palace. The vast windswept rooms were drafty. The front door opened to an atrium complete with a koi pond, and that was grand and all, but not as practical as you'd think. At the end of a long day, where did you toss your shoes and drop your purse? What if you stumbled in at two in the morning and fell into the pond? Sofia looked around for a surface to lean on. There were none.

Sofia said, "It's kinda empty, though…"

"Don't worry. We're having the entire house staged. That's going to set us back, but I think it's worth it."

They weren't alone in the twenty-two-million-dollar house. A photographer was snapping photos in the kitchen and, out in the yard, an insect-shaped drone was buzzing about. "For aerial footage," Leila had explained. "Our buyer could be a Russian oligarch or a Hollywood producer. The property has to show well online."

"When was it built?" Sofia asked as tactfully as she could. Despite the retractable this and that and the outstanding views, the house didn't read modern to her.

"In the nineties," Leila replied. "I know, it's basically a teardown, but it comes with approved plans from a cool French architect. *Très chic.*"

"Twenty-two million for a teardown?" Sofia commented.

Leila explained that the price was low for Star Island. "We're basically selling the land."

"Then why waste your money staging it?" Sofia asked.

"If everyone who walks through those retractable doors knows the deal, what's the point?"

Leila looked doubtful. "Don't you think it needs a little something?"

Sofia looked around. All that gleaming polished terrazzo reminded her of a showroom. It was actually a pretty good space to display art.

"We could team with a gallery," Sofia proposed. "Turn this floor into an indoor–outdoor sculpture garden. We throw a fabulous party, invite the art scene, every dealer, collector and artist trending on Instagram. We lure the bloggers and the press. Last minute, we invite the top brokers and developers, as if you're doing *them* a favor."

Leila snapped her fingers. "I like your thinking. You should take a staycation more often. That's the most creative idea you've had all year."

In a cherry-red wrap dress, Leila was practically the Pinterest poster child of a well-balanced life. And Sofia, at last in a good place, no longer resented her for it.

Once the insect drone had moved on to the front yard, they ventured out to the deck. The long and slender pool was sexy in the way it curved along the bay. Sofia closed her eyes and imagined the possibilities.

"How's Jon?" Leila asked.

"He's so good," Sofia replied, without thinking.

"That answers almost all of my questions," Leila said.

"I mean…he's a good person," Sofia stammered.

Leila frowned. "Here I thought setting you up in the house would've done it. I'm disappointed. What a waste of sexual chemistry."

Sofia slipped on her sunglasses, desperate for cover. "You think we have chemistry?"

"Let's just say if anyone strikes a match near you two," Leila said, "it'll start a wildfire to ravage the Everglades."

"Okay, you got me!" Sofia was walking-on-clouds happy and didn't want to hide it. "Jon and I are a thing."

Leila celebrated the news with a shout. When she calmed down, she said, "You've got a lot of unpacking to do, young lady."

"Can't we skip that part?" Sofia asked.

"Sorry! I don't make the rules," Leila said. "You're the star of the telenovela now."

Not too long ago, Sofia had been hungry for the details of Leila's private life, the ups and downs, twists and turns of her soap-style relationship. Now that the spotlight was on her, the glare was giving her a headache. Sofia had no choice but to indulge her public. She fed some details to Leila, including the trip to Key West. When she was done, Leila glared at her, more pissed than anything.

"Let me get this straight," Leila said. "You told Merci and her friends before me?"

"They ambushed me!" Sofia cried. "I had no choice."

"I'm out of the loop. How am I out of the loop?"

"There's no loop."

"You told Nick that you split up with Franco *weeks* before telling me."

"That was in the heat of the moment, and I'm sorry."

Leila rested her elbows on the rail. "Everyone is keeping things from me."

"What are you talking about?" Sofia asked.

"I get the sense Nick's hiding something," Leila replied.

"Knowing Nick, it's probably work stuff," Sofia said. "The man has a one-track mind."

"The last time he hid 'work stuff' from me, he was moving to another state."

Sofia wrote this off as nonsense. "He bought a house! He's not going anywhere."

Leila gave her a look as if to ask how she could be so

naive. But Sofia was clear. She had no idea how things would work out with Jon, but she was sure Nick loved Leila.

Leila turned to her with a gleam in her eyes. "Please tell me Jon's as good as I think he is."

There were things Sofia would not share. This wasn't one of them. "He is…amazing."

"Yes!" Leila balled her fists and punched the air. "I love it! You two are so cool together."

Leila's opinion mattered. Hadn't she determined that she and Franco were no good together? On that subject, Sofia had a follow-up question. "Why did you think Franco and I weren't a good fit?"

Leila slid her an anxious look. "Aren't we done with that?"

Sofia bristled. "We're done! Yes, but—"

Leila wouldn't back down. "But what?"

"But what did you see that I didn't?" Sofia asked.

How had Leila been so sure? Sofia hadn't seen the red flags until it was too late. What if she made the same mistake with Jon?

"You were different around him," Leila said. "We'd have so much fun when he wasn't around. But whenever he joined us, you were tense. You two bickered a lot."

Sofia took mental notes. *Tension. Bickering.*

"You and Jon get along," Leila said. "It isn't forced. I noticed it from day one. And you look so happy now."

Sofia nodded. She had discovered a lazy, happy side of herself that she liked.

Leila took her time before saying anything more. Sofia got the sense that she was weighing her words. "You've always been so serious, Sofia. Why not live a little? Don't worry about the future. Relax and have some *fun*."

There was that word again.

The word dogged Sofia, long after she'd returned to her office. *Serious* was just another way of saying *boring*, wasn't it? She mulled it over during a meeting with Ericka. Her associate of five years had put in a formal request to take over the private-event arm of the business, mainly the baby showers, office parties and bachelorette bashes.

"This would lighten your load," Ericka said. "Leaving you free to pursue real estate and corporate clients."

"This new expanded role comes with a raise, I guess?" Sofia asked.

"Yes," Ericka said. "And commission for every new client I bring in."

Ericka had joined her team straight after graduating from FIU's hospitality program. She'd paid her dues. If Sofia wanted to keep her, she'd have to promote her.

"Think about it," Ericka said before leaving her office.

Sofia promised she would, and went right back to thinking about the things she and Leila had discussed.

Why had she been so eager to wrap things up with Jon? As soon as they'd left Mile Marker behind, Sofia had started planning an exit strategy. She'd been so determined to make a clean break. It was as if a day or two of fun was all she could handle. Boring.

Sofia took a meeting with a local charity for elderly protection looking to throw an unconventional fundraiser. Then she spent the afternoon researching art galleries, particularly the lesser-known spots in the outskirts of Wynwood. Shortly before closing time, Miguel stopped by with a few things she'd asked for. Sofia took inventory: three work dresses, a pair of heels and her heavy-duty makeup bag. Just enough for a week or so. She had no intention of staying with Jon indefinitely, but what was the harm in lingering a while?

"You forgot my perfume," she said.

"I'm not your personal assistant," Miguel said.

"I know, and I thanked you ten times."

Miguel had their father's brown-sugar complexion and watery green eyes, but none of his easy personality. He was cranky and easily excitable. Like Sofia, though, he worked hard. After all, he'd grown their dad's construction business, expanding from Miami-Dade County to Broward and Palm Beach.

Sofia had inherited their grandmother's house in lower Biscayne. Back then, the neighborhood was gritty, seedy, but ripe for gentrification. Now dubbed the Upper East Side, previously neglected properties had morphed over time into trendy showrooms, storefronts and yoga studios. And today, when Sofia looked out of her ground-level office window, there were no iron bars to mask the view. She had made very few changes to the typical Florida bungalow. Black-and-white striped awnings punched up the plain facade. The pink neon sign hanging above the door read POP MIAMI.

Miguel plopped onto the seat facing her desk, in no apparent hurry to leave.

"When are the folks coming back?" he asked.

Sofia sorted through a pile of mail. "Sunday the twenty-fifth. You're picking them up at the airport, right?"

He nodded, and looked around her office. It wasn't the spectacular suite that Jon enjoyed in his glass tower but it was, in its way, very stylish. She'd paired an antique mahogany desk with a modern upholstered chair. The walls were crammed with black-and-white photos of her team hard at work at various events. The view from her window wasn't as serene as the bay. The lively and ever-changing Biscayne Boulevard was interesting, all the same.

"Are you camping out in your office?" Miguel asked.

"No," she replied nervously. "I'm staying with a friend. How's Little Red Fish, by the way?"

"I forgot to feed it on Tuesday, but it's fine."

"Miguel!"

She expected her little fish to be alive when she got back, whenever that was. She'd bought it at a pet shop across the street the week she'd moved in with her brother, lonely for companionship. It reminded her of a fish she'd won at the fair back in grade school.

"I don't have pets for a reason," Miguel said.

"Just feed it. That's all I ask."

"Just give me your address, that's all I ask," he said.

"What? Why?" Last Sofia had checked, she was a grown woman.

"In case you turn up in the trunk of some psycho's car. Someone ought to know where you are, Sofia."

Put that way, he had a point. Not that Jon was a murderous psycho, but a girl could have other reasons for firing a flare gun. Like heartbreak. She grabbed a pen and jotted the address on a sticky note. By now, she knew it by heart.

Miguel folded the note into his wallet. "One last thing."

Sofia knew instinctively what that one last thing would be.

"Have you heard from Franco?" he asked.

"We don't keep in touch," she said tightly.

"I know things aren't great between you two, but you can't just drop him. You know?"

"I don't know." Sofia set aside the pile of mail that hadn't required sorting in the first place. "And I believe he dropped me first."

"Who cares?" Miguel asked. "Water under the bridge. He's in real trouble now."

"I care. Plus, he's got good lawyers."

"Last I spoke to him, he sounded kind of confused."

"I wouldn't worry. I'm sure his attorney will set him straight."

Sofia got up and ushered Miguel toward the door, thanking him for the eleventh time for dropping off her stuff. It was quitting time, and her evening did not include worrying about whether Franco understood his legal defense strategy.

"He didn't do it, Sofia," Miguel said, one foot out the door. "He's not a crook."

Sofia let out a long haggard breath. "I know. That's why I helped with the lawyer. And I trust he'll be cleared, but I can't hold his hand through it. Okay?"

Miguel nodded but left looking unconvinced.

Sofia locked up her office and took the causeway to Miami Beach, her new commute already familiar. She let herself in with her key and headed straight to the bedroom. For the sake of spontaneity and fun, she did what she'd been convinced she'd never do. She stripped down to her lace panties, posed and took a selfie.

Chapter 17

For the first time in his professional career, Jon wished the day away. He was bored, and it wasn't for lack of work. One of his clients had been accused of bribing Brazilian politicians to secure local contracts. Another was facing investment fraud charges. Jon was preparing for trial, but advising his client to settle. This was the juicy part. And yet, he was restless in his meetings. When he checked his phone, it wasn't for message updates but to keep his eye on the clock, wondering when Sofia would make it home. *Home.*

At five on the dot, he shut off his computer, ready to bolt, when Stephanie called asking for a quick meeting.

"I've got some updates on the Francisco Ramirez case," she said. "It's been a busy day and there've been some developments."

He offered her a seat. "Let's hear it."

"So it would appear, on top of everything else, the company omitted a source of income," Stephanie said.

Jon swore under his breath.

"It seems to me his associate was running a shadow business from the dealership. We're talking about used auto parts."

It boiled down to this: Franco's partner, Steven Pike, sold after-market car parts. He mostly insisted on cash payments, but a few clients had paid by check and reported the expense in their tax returns.

"Not only did he omit a source of income," Stephanie said, "there's evidence he collected and pocketed over twenty grand in sales taxes over the years."

"I'm supposed to believe Ramirez had nothing to do with this."

"Honestly, Ramirez was a partner in name only. He was brought in as the company's young and hip spokesperson, but was encouraged to leave the accounting to Steve Pike."

"That's all good, but they'll go for conspiracy."

"I know," Stephanie said.

"Make sure he's turned over every bank account, every piggy bank. If he's stashed cash in his mattress—"

"I'll find it myself," Stephanie said.

"That's what I want to hear," Jon said.

She was the newest member of the economic crime division that he and another partner headed. He knew she was eager to prove herself, but he appreciated her zeal... and her patience with him. "Thanks, Stephanie."

"You got it."

Jon grabbed his keys and patted his pockets for his wallet.

"Aren't you going to Terry's retirement party?" Stephanie asked. "It's starting now."

Terry was the mail clerk and a sweetheart. If Jon skipped the party, she'd be offended. He figured he'd stop by for a minute on his way out. But when he got to the conference room, the senior partner was mid-speech. Jon took a seat in the back of the room. He went to silence his phone when a text message from Sofia popped up. He tapped on it.

Holy mother...

The phone's display framed a woman's bare body. Her face had been partially cropped from the shot, but he didn't need to see her face to recognize his Sofia. The deep tan skin paled where her bathing suit had hid her from him. Her breasts were full and the nipples a deep rich brown.

He traced the slope of her waistline and the curve of her hips. Her navel shaped like a cherry, and between her thighs was a bit of red lace.

Jon pocketed his phone and pinched the bridge of his nose.

He couldn't leave now. He couldn't get up from his seat.

The house was quiet. Her heels were in the foyer and her tailored jacket draped over a dining table chair. Jon tossed his jacket over hers and tensed at the sound of her voice from upstairs.

"You're home early," she said.

She was sitting on the top of the stairs just as she had been in the picture, hair piled on the top of her head, breasts round and heavy, golden-brown legs crossed at the ankles.

Jon was going to die.

He cleared his throat. "I had an incentive."

She pulled a pin from her hair and let the rough curls tumble to her shoulders. He stood at the foot of the stairs in quiet admiration of the woman he loved. Thousands of pieces snapped together—every coincidental encounter, every decision he'd made since meeting her—giving him a complete picture of his future and her role in it. She colored his world. He never wanted to be without her. But this wasn't the time for heartfelt confessions.

Jon charged the stairs. Sofia hopped onto her bare feet and raced to the bedroom. He caught her easily, scooped her up and dropped her onto their bed. She cried out when he bit down on her panties and tugged.

One way or the other, the bit of red lace was coming off.

Midnight. Jon threw open the closet door and noticed straight away extra dresses hanging on one side and new shoes on the storage shelf. To put things mildly, he was ecstatic. He stepped out to question Sofia. She was in bed, fresh from a shower, and watching him closely. Under her loose white T-shirt—*his* loose white T-shirt—her chest rose and fell with the roll of a breath. Was it possible that the woman who'd sent him a sexy selfie in the middle of the workday was worried a couple of dresses in his closet was too bold a move?

"Come on," he said. "You've got more than two pairs of shoes and a handful of dresses."

"That's plenty for now," she said.

"If you say so."

He went into the closet for a pair of sweatpants. When he came out, she hadn't moved.

"It's not like I'm moving in," she said.

He approached the bed and rested a knee on the corner. "But for convenience's sake, maybe consider bringing in a few more things you need. It's a big closet. You're not crowding me."

She hesitated. "There's something."

Jon tied the drawstring at the waist of his pants. "Yes?"

"A fish," she said. "My brother isn't feeding it. I'd take it to the office but I'm not always there."

"What kind of fish?" he asked.

"Betta. A fighter."

He liked the sound of that. "What color?"

"Red," she said curtly.

"Just one fish?" he asked. "Not an aquarium full?"

She narrowed her eyes at him. "Forget I said anything."

Jon would not forget. This was too good to let go. "What kind of pet is a fish?" he asked.

"The kind that doesn't need to be walked or fixed or trained or anything!" she cried, exasperated.

"Did you win him at a county fair?" he asked.

"Jon!" She grabbed a pillow and tossed it at him. "I swear to God, I'm sorry I said anything."

He caught the pillow and tossed it onto the floor. "Bring the fish. What's his name? Or is it a she?"

"It's an *it*. I don't know what *it* is. I think *it*'s pretty."

"Like I think you're pretty?" he asked.

"I bet that works with some women," she said.

"I bet that works with you, too."

She was blushing prettily. He fell onto the bed and rested his head on her lap.

"Listen," he said. "Bring the fish, a few more clothes and a couple of more shoes, and we've got a deal."

She ran a finger down the length of his nose. "I don't want to bicker about this."

"Who's bickering?" he asked. "This is a negotiation."

"Okay then," she said. "All I want is to bring one fish into the house and not have it be weird."

"We're past weird, and this isn't about the fish."

"What's it about?" she asked quietly.

Jon reached under her T-shirt and dragged his knuckles along the arch of her back. "You being comfortable here. That's what it's about."

She looked doubtful, and Jon wasn't sure he'd gotten through to her. But the next day when he got home from work, there was a fish bowl on the kitchen counter and a small suitcase in the foyer.

He joined Sofia on the living room couch. Her computer was open on her lap.

"It's male," he said. "The male betta has longer fins. And yes, it's pretty."

She folded the laptop shut, a little smile tugging at her lips. "You've done your research."

"Wikipedia is a hell of a tool." He stripped off his jacket and dropped it on the coffee table. "Fun fact—males and females are kept apart until breeding time."

"They can't live together," she said.

"They'd kill each other," he said.

She nodded knowingly and set the laptop aside.

Jon slipped a hand between her legs. "Thank God we're not fish."

Chapter 18

Sofia wrapped up a conference call with Nick and Leila. The Star Island open house was scheduled for Saturday. Five modern art galleries had signed up to show their most provocative sculptures. The night would end with a silent auction. Nick said he was concerned the artwork would steal the guests' attention away from the house. Sofia proposed to work with a consultant and display only pieces that would enhance the house's architecture rather than compete with it. When he still expressed doubts, Sofia thought it best to move the discussion away from art.

"Think of it like this," Sofia said. "If we can lure in fifty social media stars with the promise of interesting content, the free publicity they'll generate will be worth it. Star Island will be trending overnight."

"I trust you, Sofia," Nick said.

"When have I ever let you down?" Sofia asked.

After Nick got off the call, Sofia and Leila chatted for a while. Then Leila abruptly asked if Sofia would rather rent or own.

"What do you mean?" Sofia asked.

"How long do you plan to live with Miguel?" Leila pressed.

Sofia had moved in with Franco straight out of college—and had soon regretted it. She should've lived alone for a while. And now, she was playing house with Jon.

Sofia confessed. "I'm not living with Miguel. I *am*, but I'm not."

"Please don't tell me you're still at Jon's," Leila said.

"I'm still at Jon's."

"Holy crap!" Sofia heard Leila drop the phone and call out, presumably to Nick. "She's living with Jon! You were right!"

Sofia didn't catch Nick's muffled response, but Leila laughed before picking up the phone again.

"I hate the both of you," Sofia said drily. "Some things are private!"

"Don't worry. Nick is discreet. And by the way," Leila whispered now, "I still think he's keeping something from me. He's acting shadier than ever. Last night, I went through his desk looking for stamps. The man turned three shades of red. I had to walk away."

"Have you tried talking to him?" Sofia asked. That would seem like the obvious thing to do.

"Yes, and he said there's nothing going on."

Sofia picked up a pink stress-relief ball with her company's logo and rolled it between her palms. "Maybe there's nothing going on, Leila."

"Yeah, like there's nothing between you and your new live-in boyfriend."

"Jon's not my boyfriend," Sofia said. "He's just a guy I'm having fun with for the time being."

"Just a guy? Is that what we're going with?" Leila said. "Okay. Got it."

"Okay. Good."

As soon as she got off the phone with Leila, it rang again. She answered and Jon's raspy voice filled her ear.

"I miss you," he said.

"That's not possible!" She laughed. "We were up half the night talking."

"Now I want to stay up doing something else," he said. "You should feel me right now."

"Jon…" Sofia squeezed the stress ball until her knuckles turned white.

"Do you miss me?" he asked.

"I do now."

"I left so early this morning, I didn't get to see you dressed," he said. "What are you wearing?"

"Not that old line," she teased.

She got up from her desk and walked over to her office door to lock it. No way did she want anyone barging in.

"I'll guess. One of those tight skirts?"

Her back to the door, Sofia nodded her response.

"Do me a favor," he said. "Wiggle your skirt up over your thighs."

"Oh, my God, Jon," she whispered.

"Is that too much to ask, Sofia?"

He said her name quietly. She heard the dark promise in his voice, the one that he fulfilled each and every time. Already her fingers were grabbing at the thick cotton of her skirt and dragging the hem up and along her thighs to her hips.

He asked what she was wearing underneath. "Satin or lace?"

"Lace." Her fingers traced the intricate pattern.

"I should've known," he said. "Black or red?"

"Blue."

"Blue like the sky or the bay?"

Sofia imagined him at his office window, trying to match the color of her delicates to the view before him, and it drove her crazy. Heat poured between her legs.

"Never mind," he said. "I've got to go."

"Jon!" She couldn't have been more shaken if someone had dowsed her with ice water. "What do you mean? Where are you going?"

"I've got a meeting."

"Don't you dare hang up this phone!"

She heard him laugh. "Sofia, I'm at work."

"*I'm* at work!" she yelled.

How dare he call her, whip her into this state and hang up? She swore she'd never take his calls again.

"Meet me for lunch," he said. "Twelve-thirty."

"Where?" She hated herself for being so damn easy.

"Where do you think?" he asked. "Oh, and Sofia?"

"What?" She snapped, frustrated with him—with herself—and just plain sexually frustrated.

"Don't touch what's mine."

Noon on the dot, Sofia was in her car. Testing the sport mode for the first time, she flew along the causeway toward the beach. When traffic built up, as it always did, she tapped the wheel restlessly. "Come on! Come on! Come on!"

She pulled up to the gate just as Jon's car came tearing down Alton from the opposite direction, blowing the red light at the intersection. The gate took forever to open, inch by inch, revealing their tropical hideaway. She pulled into the driveway, and he pulled in behind her. Sofia jumped out of her car, just as his car door swung open.

"You better run!" he called out.

Squealing like a child losing at tag, she scrambled to the front door and fumbled with her keys. Jon caught her, held her, his hands exploring her everywhere. She softened in his arms, but he warned her to open the door or else he'd rip off her blouse right there. Sofia twisted the key in the lock and the door finally gave way.

They stumbled together into the foyer. Between kisses,

Sofia lashed out. "You're terrible! How could you toy with me like that?"

"Payback." Jon stepped away from her and peeled off his suit jacket. The lining was a gorgeous plum. "I was in a room full of people when you sent that sexy pic. I couldn't get up from the table for a long time."

"I was flirting! What you did today was mean."

"Malicious," he said, and pinned her against the wall. "I like how that sounds."

He gripped the waist of her skirt and tried to work it down. When that didn't work, he tried the other end and hiked the hem up.

"Well, never again," Sofia said.

"I don't believe it. You love to up the ante." He fell to his knees, and she heard him suck in his breath before he gazed up at her. "Blue like the sky."

Sofia shrugged out of her blouse and let it fall to the floor, showing him the pretty lace bra that matched the panties he had been so eager to see.

"Did you do as you were told?" he asked.

Sofia cupped his upturned face. "What do you mean?"

He took hold of her hands and kissed the palms, the fingertips. "Did you touch what's mine?"

Malicious…

"It's not yours until you make it yours," she said.

Jon laughed quietly. "You're a brave woman."

Sofia was going to fire back something clever, but he swept her off her feet and carried her up the stairs.

Sofia was on a high. There was no use returning to the office. She left a new client meeting to Ericka, her new private events coordinator, and spent the afternoon browsing the aisles of her favorite party supply warehouse, prepping for the charity fundraiser confirmed for next month. Sofia had proposed a risqué bingo night to raise money for the Women for Elder Protection. Hunky topless waiters would serve cocktails and a gorgeous drag queen MC would host the event. After an hour of unfocused browsing, she purchased a case of beaded necklaces. The guests could play bingo for beads, Mardi Gras style. On her way out, she caught her reflection on a mirrored surface. There it was: a smile of intense satisfaction that she couldn't wipe off her face. What had Jon done to her?

Still grappling with an answer to that question, Sofia ran into Nick in the parking lot.

"Hey! What are you doing on my turf?" she asked.

The warehouse bordered the river and wasn't too far from the courthouse where she and Jon had had jury duty. It wasn't the most glamorous part of town, and Maserati drivers such as Nick seldom came around.

"Hate to break it to you, but you're literally on my turf. I own the building."

"You own my warehouse?"

"As of last week."

"What's going to happen to it?" Sofia demanded. She'd been coming to this wholesaler for years.

Nick kicked the rear tires of his black sports car, gauging the pressure. "The lease is up at the end of the year. Then they move to Opa-Locka."

"Way out there!" Sofia cried.

He shrugged. "Sorry, babe."

"What do you want with this property anyway?" she asked.

He explained that Miami's rental market was screwed up and he intended to fix that. "We're two miles away from three major hospitals. Not to mention the local public defender and state attorney's offices."

"Don't forget the courthouse."

"You're helping to make my point," Nick said. "There's no place decent in the area for all those young doctors and lawyers to live."

Sofia acknowledged his plan made sense. "Does Leila know?"

He gave her a quizzical look, blue eyes darkening, and Sofia immediately regretted having asked the question.

"Of course she knows," he said. "She picked the spot. You might've told her it was your favorite warehouse."

"It never came up."

A dusty white Land Rover pulled into the parking lot and moments later Nick introduced her to the architect hired to transform the boxy warehouse into a modern ten-story apartment building.

"Tell your dad and Miguel to put in a bid when the time comes," Nick said.

"Will do," Sofia said, and wished both men a good day. She was fitting the crate of beaded necklaces into the trunk of her car when Nick asked the architect to give them a minute.

"Why would you ask me about Leila? What did she say to you?" Nick asked her.

"Oh, that... Forget I said anything," Sofia said. "I don't want to get involved."

"Forget that," Nick said. "I've kept secrets for you, Sofia."

"And I regret putting you in that position."

"Too bad," Nick retorted. "That's the position we're in. Now tell me. What did Leila say to you?"

What could she do? If she tried to get away, she'd likely have to drive over Nick's body. The man obviously didn't play around when it came to Leila.

"She thinks you're hiding something."

Her revelation didn't trouble Nick nearly as much as

she'd feared. After the initial surprise faded, he let out a low laugh. "That woman knows me so well."

"So you are hiding something?" Sofia asked.

"A three-carat diamond ring."

Oh, my God! "You're going to propose?"

"I've been trying to."

"It's not that hard," Sofia said. "You get down on one knee and ask."

"I want to do it in the new house," Nick said. "The renovations are taking forever. The whole thing is throwing me off."

Sofia's heart melted. This was the best news she'd heard in a long time. "Why the house? Take her to dinner or—"

"No," Nick said firmly. "I fell in love with that woman in that house. It'll mean something to her if I do it there."

The story of the house was also the story of their love affair. Back when Leila had first started as his assistant, the house was the very first they'd sold together as a team. Sofia had helped organize a small-scale open house. When the house went back on the market one year later and was in bad need of repairs, Nick scooped it up. Now he planned to propose to Leila in the renovated space for the ultimate storybook conclusion.

So this is how it is when a man loves a woman, Sofia thought. *He's eager to propose.* She'd had to browbeat Franco. When he'd finally gotten down on one knee on the grainy sand of a beach in Key Largo, it had felt as if she'd scripted the whole thing.

Nick reached out and raised her chin with a finger. "Are you crying?"

Sofia swatted his hand away and climbed into her car. "Just make it memorable," she said through the open window. "Leila deserves the whole shebang. She deserves fireworks!"

Nick vetoed the fireworks. "She'd prefer candlelight. You better stock up on candles. When the time comes, I'm going to need your help."

Chapter 19

When Jon called her at work on Thursday, Sofia steeled herself. She wouldn't fall for the same trick twice. But just in case she did, she asked Melissa to leave her office.

"You're not allowed to call me at work anymore," she said.

It took him a moment to catch on and when he did, his laughter rang hollow.

"Is something wrong?" she asked.

"Damn, you know me well. How can you tell?"

"I don't know," Sofia said. "I'm just guessing."

Isn't that what Nick had said about Leila? Something about her knowing him well? And Sofia knew how deeply Leila loved Nick; the man was her heart. She couldn't be falling in love with Jon. Falling in love was the opposite of fun. Panicking, Sofia scanned her desktop for her stress ball. It was nowhere to be found, so she ripped a sheet of paper from a notepad and crumpled it.

"My stepfather died this morning."

"Oh, my God." Sofia put her panic attack on pause. She hadn't expected that. "Jon, I'm sorry."

Family drama was her thing. How ironic that tragedy had struck in his court.

"Kidney failure," he said. "He was on dialysis for the last year and a half. I had no idea. That's the kind of ass I am."

"You're not...you're not an ass."

"That's what they all think."

He explained that his leaving home to join his father, only weeks after his stepdad had moved in, had long been perceived as a slight. His mother resented him for rejecting the home she'd worked hard to give him. His stepdad had only pretended not to care.

"I don't see it that way," Sofia said. "Parents share custody all the time and—"

"Hold on, sweetheart. Give me a second."

Jon had never called her by an endearment. Instead, he breathed life into her name and she'd always loved it. People tossed around "sweetheart" all the time, but the way he said it made it special. She wished he hadn't said it over the phone. She wanted to see his face.

Sofia's heart, sugar sweet in her chest, was crumbling like day-old cake. She cradled the phone to her ear and listened to the fragmented conversation Jon was having with his assistant. He was making travel arrangements. *Flight 2810 is full. First-class only? Go ahead. Book it. And get me a room at the W. Might as well be comfortable.* He was leaving. That made sense. There'd be a funeral. There'd be family obligations. But she didn't want him to go.

"I won't be coming home tonight," he said, returning to their conversation. "The funeral is in the morning and I've got to be in Hoboken, New Jersey."

"When will you be back?" she asked.

"Sunday."

A static silence filled the space between them.

"I'm heading to the airport," he said, bridging that silence.

"Now? Don't you have to pack? You'll need a good suit, a change of underwear." Why did she sound like a wife? Seriously, though, someone had to fuss over him. He lived such an isolated life. When life got rough, who was in his corner? He claimed to be close to his dad, but their only connection—as far as she could tell—was a nightstand drawer full of postcards.

"I've got a suit here," he said. "And a gym bag full of clean underwear."

She smiled at his unfailing wit. She summoned all her courage to squeak out the next few words. "I'll miss you."

"Will you be there when I get back?" he asked.

Tears sprang to Sofia's eyes. Where else would she be? "Yes, Jon. And I'll want to hear all about Hoboken."

"I won't bore you with that story," he said.

Sofia sat very still at her desk long after Jon had said goodbye. She couldn't believe the thoughts she was entertaining. She couldn't believe what she was about to do. She called Melissa back into her office, not believing what she was about to say.

"Do me a favor, please? Get me a seat on Flight 2810 to Hoboken."

"Hoboken, *New Jersey*?" Melissa asked, confused.

"Is there another one?" She got up and offered the girl her seat. "Use my computer. I've got to put together a travel bag."

"How long will you be away?" Melissa asked.

"One night."

In a corner of her office, an antique armoire held a small collection of clothes for quick changes when going home was not an option. She had a couple of plain black dresses to choose from. Jon didn't like her in black, but she couldn't show up at a funeral in canary yellow. And like Jon, she had a gym bag with a change of underwear, deodorant and shampoo. Was it enough? She'd pick up more stuff at the airport.

"There's an American Airlines Flight 2810 from Miami to JFK airport," Melissa said after a quick search.

"When does it leave?"

"At two. It's eleven-thirty now," Melissa said. "You'd have to leave for the airport right away."

"That's the one," Sofia said.

Melissa clicked around a bit and said regretfully, "The flight is full. First-class only."

"Book it. I've got miles."

Sofia folded the dresses into her gym bag. Attending the funeral wasn't the important thing, she told herself while selecting the perfect pair of funeral pumps. She could wait for Jon at the hotel and make sure he didn't spend all his time feeling guilty for supposedly being an ass of a stepson.

A couple more clicks of the mouse and Melissa said, "All that's left is an aisle seat."

"Book it, Melissa."

Window or aisle was irrelevant in first-class.

Sofia was the last passenger to board the plane. She spotted Jon right away at a window seat. He made for a ruggedly elegant traveler in his light gray suit, staring out the little oval window, his expression somber. By the look in the attendant's eyes as she led Sofia to his row and the empty seat next to his, it was clear she thought Sofia had won the jackpot of travel companions.

Sofia cleared her throat to get his attention. She hadn't considered his reaction to her crashing his trip. She'd only considered her own need to be there for him. Now she worried he might think she was crazy. He looked up and their eyes locked. His expression was guarded, and after only a second, she lost her nerve.

She could run off the plane…

"Ma'am, please take your seat."

…and never fly American again.

Jon got up and took the gym bag from Sofia's hands. He brushed past her to lift it into the overhead compartment.

Then he took her by the waist and guided her into the seat he'd vacated, taking the aisle seat for himself.

Sofia swallowed hard. How could she think he'd ever reject her?

She turned to him, her voice shaky. "The thing to do is order food. When my uncle died a few of years ago, there was never enough food in the house."

"Is that the thing to do?" he asked wryly.

"Yes," she said. "Nobody needs flowers. What they need is food."

He reached over to fasten her seat belt. She rested her hands on his larger stronger ones, wanting to be strong for him.

Leila called while Jon was at the front desk trying to upgrade their standard hotel room to a suite.

"Quick question," Leila said. "Brie and I were considering a signature cocktail for Saturday night. We could invent something and call it the Star Island Star or maybe just go with the classic Sex on the Beach. What do you think?"

"Can't really think right now," Sofia whispered into the phone. "I'm in Hoboken."

"What in the world?" Leila said.

Sofia crossed the sultry lobby. Its dim lights and pulsing music set a mood that was at odds with the purpose of their stay. She took a seat in a club chair underneath a sculptural modern chandelier.

"Jon's stepdad died," she said. "The funeral is in the morning."

"Poor Jon!" Leila cried.

Sofia reassured her that he was holding up okay, but she had some choice words about the so-called signature cocktail. "Nix it! This is not a rooftop party at the Clevelander.

I've already consulted with a master sommelier. We'll have champagne and the best wine selection."

"You think you'll be back in time?" Leila asked tentatively.

"I'm flying home tomorrow night," Sofia replied. "Jon will stay on."

Leila mocked her. "You flew to New Jersey for one night? What a supportive girlfriend you are!"

"I'm not his girlfriend."

"Of course not," Leila said. "You flew to Hoboken for the funeral of your hookup's stepdad, as one does."

Jon was done at the front desk. Sofia watched as he searched around for her and saw his face light up when he spotted her. He held up a couple of key cards triumphantly. Of course, he'd gotten the upgrade. He always got his way.

After they'd checked into the hotel, Jon took Sofia to his family home. He had to dip his head to enter the house. He felt like a giant in the tight foyer. Everything was as he had ever known it. The coats and jackets hanging on pegs and shoes lined up against the wall. The framed quote "God Bless our Mess!" hung crooked on a nail. And it took him a while to recalibrate. Every visit took him to the past. He'd left this house, a boy burdened with sadness and guilt. Guilt for having made a choice that had ultimately proved to be right for him. The night before he'd moved out, his mother had hollered at him, called him ungrateful. Thanks to Sofia, he now understood that his mother's reaction might've been unbalanced.

Sofia was standing close behind him. He helped her out of the raincoat she'd purchased at the hotel boutique. It was a crappy day, perfect for a funeral. His half sister, Lena, had welcomed them at the door. She was only seventeen, and she stared at Sofia as if she were an intruder. Jon would have none of that.

"This is Sofia Silva," he said to the girl. "Make her feel welcome, please."

But he needn't have worried. Sofia quickly won her over with her engaging smile. Even his irritable mother was slightly less irritable around Sofia. They'd found his mother in the living room surrounded by friends and family. She looked tired, the lines of her face pronounced.

"Mom," Jon said.

His mind went blank. He couldn't think of one word to console her. Sofia rested a hand on his back and said, "So sorry for your loss. Jon tells me he was a great man."

Then she forced him forward, that hand on his back pushing him toward his mother. Jon hugged and kissed her. She felt small and fragile in his arms.

"Jon didn't tell me he was bringing a friend," she said.

"It was a last-minute decision," Sofia said. "And I'm here to help. Any errands, anything you need done, let me know."

"Just make yourself comfortable," his mother said, adding, "You, too, Jon. There is coffee in the kitchen."

Jon led Sofia off by the hand. For having done this for him, helping him through that two-minute interaction, he owed her for life.

Twenty-four hours flew by and it was time for Sofia to head back to Miami. The trip had gone as well as she could've hoped. She'd met Jon's family. His mother was a short stout woman with salt-and-pepper hair and crumpled brown skin. Jon looked nothing like her, and physical appearance was only the start of their differences. Where Jon was composed, never losing his temper, his mother was a loose cannon. More often than not, her children were at the receiving end of her verbal attacks. Jon's half sister, Lena, was only a teenager, grieving the loss of her father.

Early Friday morning, Sofia rode with Jon to the cemetery and they attended the simple graveside funeral together. Following the service, family and friends filled the modest suburban home and stayed well after the sandwiches Lena had prepared ran out. Thankfully, Sofia had ordered enough lasagna, garlic bread and green salad to feed an army.

Throughout the entire ordeal, Jon had held her hand. And now, he kissed her in the back of the town car waiting to whisk her to JFK.

"I don't want you to go," he whispered. "I only want to travel with you talking my ear off."

Sofia edited that down to: I only want to travel with you.

She cupped his face. "I'll be there when you get back on Sunday night."

"I'm going to miss your party."

"Don't even think about that!" she scolded.

"I wanted to be there." He closed his eyes and pressed his forehead to hers. "What am I going to do about my mother?"

The question surprised her. She hadn't realized that this was a concern. "I'm sure she doesn't need you to do anything. It'll be enough that you're here to support her."

"Since when is that ever enough?" he asked. "Should I offer money?"

At times like this, Sofia thought, money solved a lot of problems. But if he was asking whether he could use money as a substitute to connecting with his mother… "Maybe Lena can clue you in on things she might need done. Like clearing out the garage or something. Be useful. Show her you care."

"You're saying keep busy and stay out of trouble. Good

call." He winked at her, those brown eyes mischievous again.

Before he climbed out of the car, he handed a few bills to the driver and told him to take good care of her. He stood watching from the hotel entrance as the car pulled away. Sofia couldn't tear her gaze from the window until he had disappeared from sight.

She wanted to be his girlfriend. She wanted to be his everything. Admitting it ripped a hole in her safety net.

Could this really be mine?

Chapter 20

Early Saturday afternoon, Sofia drove over the Star Island Bridge. She was there to meet with the gallerists and ensure that the sculptures had been set up as planned. She was also there to make sure the koi pond had been thoroughly cleaned and the koi themselves looked healthy and spry. But really she was there to get out of the house. Where once she had enjoyed spending time alone, she could no longer bear it. She missed Jon in a borderline irrational way. The cure for that was to keep busy.

A twenty-four-million-dollar teardown house was spectacular when well lit and filled with art. The retractable doors had done the thing they were designed to: disappear. The main floor seemed to float above the bay. A quartet was setting up by the pool. Nick and Leila looked genuinely pleased as they walked around, fingers linked, taking it all in. Watching them, Sofia's heart seized. She might have burst into tears if Ericka hadn't approached with a mini crisis to solve.

When Jon got back, they'd have a talk. While reassuring the caterer that she'd have the crystal-encrusted Buddha blocking the entrance to the kitchen moved out of the way, Sofia made up her mind. She couldn't go on like this, playing house as if nothing was at stake. Everything was at stake. She didn't want to have fun. Her heart yearned for reassurances, stability. She was old-school and could only handle so much fun.

The guests arrived, wine flowed and the party took off. Feeling guilty for indulging in an anxiety attack on the job, Sofia moved to the deck to better take command. Leila made faces at her from across the yard. Sofia waved at her, but she kept on making faces. She blinked furiously, as if trying to communicate with her via telepathy. She added a gesture, discreetly pointing toward the wine bar, and mouthed, *Jon is here*.

Sofia looked around. He wasn't at the bar. He was two feet away, chatting with Brie next to an acrylic bust of Marilyn Monroe. He looked scruffy and tired. He looked sexy. Sofia felt as if she were rising off the ground and up into the starry sky.

Leila and Nick got to him first. By the looks of it, they were offering their condolences. Sofia took the time to pull herself together. She grabbed a glass of wine off a passing waiter's tray and took a few gulps. Leila was pointing to her now. Jon shook hands with Nick, kissed Leila on the cheek and came looking for her. He took the steps leading up to the deck, his eyes sweeping over her. Her body-hugging red dress was a Victoria Beckham marvel that she broke out only for big-time events. And it was worthy of admiration.

She put on a show of moderate surprise. "What are you doing back so soon?"

"If you're happy to see me, Sofia, just say so."

"I'm surprised and happy."

He pulled her to him by the waist. "I wanted to be here."

As much as she wanted him to hold her, she had to wiggle herself free. "Sorry. No PDA on the job. Company policy."

"Who owns this company?" he asked.

She held firm. "I do, but I have to set an example."

"I hear this house has eighteen bathrooms."

"Eight," she said, laughing. "It has eight bathrooms."

"Take me to one of them."

"I'll do you one better."

Sofia led him to the rooftop terrace that was off-limits for now. A clear dance floor had been installed over the pool. While a DJ set up for the after party, a bartender was stirring up a Star Island Star pineapple vodka cocktail. (The signature cocktail wasn't the worst idea she'd ever heard.) She drew him to a secluded corner. They could talk tomorrow. Tonight, she'd hide away with him and let him do to her whatever he wanted—because this part was *fun*.

Little Red Fish was swimming in tight circles, his glorious fins fanned out like wings. Sofia fed him while Jon made her "breakfast." He poured almond milk into a blender cup, added a scoop of protein powder, a chopped banana, a handful of fresh mixed berries and gave the monster mixer a whirl.

"How is that breakfast?" she asked. "I expected scrambled eggs."

He poured the smoothie into a glass and handed it to her. "Drink."

Sofia reluctantly took a sip. He waited for a reaction and when she didn't offer one, he tried coaxing it out of her. "Say you love it."

"Fine!" she said after her second sip. It wasn't as if she'd never had a smoothie before, but this one was creamy and flavorful. "I love it."

He grinned. "It's the fresh berries. Women love it."

"Who are these women?" Sofia demanded. "I hate them all."

Jon rinsed out the blender cup. "Jealous, sweetheart?"

Sofia put down her glass, walked over to him at the sink and punched him in the arm. "I think I have the right to be."

He glanced down at his sculpted biceps as if a mosquito

had landed there and flew off without even attempting a bite. "Drink up. We're going to work on that punch."

One of the first things Jon had done was have a punching bag installed in the side terrace. He tossed her a pair of gloves. Sofia stared at them for a while as if she weren't sure how they worked. The fit was loose. She did her best Rocky, punching her gloved hands together and grunting with aggression.

Jon did not seem amused. He took her by the shoulders and positioned her before the bag. "Give it your best."

Sofia eyed the stuffed vinyl cylinder hanging from the ceiling. Why should she punch it? It hadn't done anything to her? It seemed like a total waste of energy.

"Jon," she said. "I'm a lover, not a fighter."

He laughed openly at that. "Come on, Sofia. There's got to be someone you'd like to punch in the face."

Well, put that way… Sofia projected Franco's face onto the black vinyl. She swung and hit it in the jaw. *Take that!* She swung again. *You lying, sexting, tax-evading, pura vida poser!* She swung as hard as she could, huffing and puffing as she went about it. The bag bobbed about wildly. Sofia doubled over, out of breath, but proud of herself.

"How… How was that?" she asked, winded. Clearly, she had to up her cardio game.

Jon steadied the bag, and motioned for her to straighten up. With his hands on her hips, he positioned her before the bag again. He took hold of her wrists and raised her hands to the height of her chin. He tapped at her feet, easing her into a more solid stance.

"Now," he said, "strike once with your right and then your left. I want to hear a sharp rhythm. One. Two."

"Yes, sir!"

"Quiet," he said. "Now go!"

So damn serious! Since when did smacking a stuffed

vinyl bag call for such attitude? She swung. One. Two. "How's that?"

"Not great."

"Jon!" She was going to take a swing at him.

"You're not a puppy. You don't get a treat just for trying."

"A puppy?" *Did he just compare me to a dog?*

"Stop talking, calm down and focus."

It took Sofia a few breaths, but when she returned to the bag, she struck with purpose. One. Two.

"Better." He laid a hand on her belly and squeezed, forcing her to contract her abdomen muscles. "From the core this time."

Is he saying I have a gut?

"Chin up. Controlled. Go again."

This time, she applied herself, wanting nothing more than to impress him.

One! Two!

"Very good."

She swiveled around, smiling, asking for a treat. "I want a kiss."

Jon took her in his arms. "I haven't taught you a damn thing, have I?"

She shook her head. "I already knew how to count to two."

He wrapped up the boxing lesson in time to watch an English League Championship soccer game—or football match, as he put it. Sofia figured they could talk during halftime. But when the beleaguered players hobbled off the field to a 0–0 score, Jon was worked up, shouting at the TV screen. It would've been the wrong time to say, "Honey, we need to talk."

Sofia settled down. The players charged back onto the field. They were trim and light on their feet and stylish, sporting beards, shaved heads, Mohawks and even the oh-so-metrosexual man bun. The commentators made witty observations on the players' attempts to set up plays and score that ever-elusive first goal. She rested her head on Jon's lap and fell asleep, wishing every Sunday could be like this one.

After lunch, Jon took a call from work, all the while heating water for tea. "Wait a minute. Wasn't he deposed twice?" he asked.

Sofia looked up from her payroll spreadsheet. She watched, her heart skipping, as he went about in the kitchen. He held the phone cradled to his ear, brows drawn in serious focus, while pulling Sainsbury's tea bags from their wrappers.

This was her man, no question about it. Now, how to go about telling him?

Last night, when they'd had a few minutes alone at the party, he had held her, told her she looked beautiful and tangled his fingers in her hair. When they rejoined the others, the weariness of the last few days had been gone and he was himself again. He moved the heavy Buddha statue out of the caterer's way. He passed her business card to a hotel mogul client. He joked around with Brie. But she couldn't shake the feeling that he had been close to telling her something important, and the opportunity had been lost.

Jon walked over, handed her a cup of tea, tousled her hair and stepped out to the yard to continue barking at his caller. She looked into her cup and admired the rich caramel color, dark tea and milk mixed just right. Her phone rang, shattering the moment. It was her parents calling from the airport in Atlanta, waiting to board their flight to Miami.

"We went to the Vatican, darling!" her mother exclaimed.

Sofia laughed. "Mom, I booked the trip, remember?"

She and Miguel had chipped in to offer their parents the

trip of a lifetime, although Sofia had been afraid it would be too much of a strain on her mother. Life was short, her mother had reminded her. She'd always dreamed of visiting the Vatican. Who was to say she could afford to postpone the trip another five years?

"It was divine," her mother carried on. "But we're glad we're coming home."

Sofia was glad, too. But in a way, their return brought back the burdens of the past. With them gone, she'd had the space and freedom to try a new life. Now, she suddenly felt less free.

"Corazón," her dad said. "It's your dad."

"I know, Dad." Who else could it be?

"What's the situation with Franco?" he asked straight away. "Cheating the IRS is serious business, *niñita*."

Usually, her father wasn't this tender. The profusion of endearments was his stab at diplomacy. Still, it touched her heart.

"It's not the IRS. It's the Florida Department—"

"Whatever it is, it's serious, Sofia!"

"Everything is under control," Sofia said. "I wouldn't worry."

"Did you speak to the lawyer?" he asked. "You know that boy isn't so bright. If he were, he wouldn't be in this mess."

Was it her responsibility to clean up the mess?

"Listen, you two," she said, figuring they had her on speakerphone so everyone at their airport gate could listen in. "You've been traveling. You're tired. We'll talk about this at home."

As soon as she got her parents off her phone, the landline rang. Sofia got up from the couch and checked the caller ID. The caller was at the gate. She wasn't expecting anyone. Jon was still outside, pacing and talking animatedly.

She answered. "Hello. Who's this?"

"Sofia, it's me. Franco."

Sofia leaned against the nearest wall. "What are you doing here?"

"Let me in. I need to speak with you."

She punched the code to the gate, then raced to the front door. He could come into the yard, but no farther. She wouldn't allow him to step foot into the house. This was an absolute invasion of her privacy and she intended to let him know it.

Franco hopped out of his black Mustang, whipped off his sunglasses and assessed the house. "Nice digs."

"How did you find me?" she asked flatly.

"Miguel gave me the address."

The traitor!

Franco strode up the path to the front door, but Sofia blocked him.

"Can I come in?" he asked.

"No. What's so urgent you couldn't have called?"

"You don't answer my calls."

"What's so urgent you couldn't have sent a text? I would've answered a text."

"Really, Sofia, can't we get out of the heat and talk?"

"No!"

The door Franco was eyeing swung open and Jon's massive body filled the doorway. The look on his face! Sofia knew this day would come. The day she'd watch helpless as her worlds finally collided. To avoid any casualties, Sofia went to Jon, rested a hand on his arm and spoke as gently as she could manage. "Could you give us a minute?"

He looked so confused that she wondered if she'd asked the question in Mandarin. She rephrased her request. "Jon, please. Give us a minute."

He stepped back into the house and shut the door without saying a word. Why did she feel as if she were betraying him? All she was asking was for some space to deal with Franco—to get rid of him, frankly. She couldn't do that with him glaring at her from the door.

Sofia turned back to the intruder. The look on his face rivaled Jon's, but less intimidating.

"You're living with my lawyer?" he asked, incredulous. "You're sleeping with him?"

"He's not your lawyer," Sofia replied.

"Can't he get disbarred for that?" Franco asked.

"Franco, Jon is not your lawyer," Sofia said through gritted teeth. "You'd be lucky if he was. Now what do you want? Why are you here?"

Franco cleared his throat. "My parents are in town, and I said you'd come by the condo this afternoon."

"Why?" she asked.

"They're panicking. They think my life's falling apart. I need you to come over and talk with them. They trust you."

So, it really was her job to clean up his mess.

"I'm not going over there," she said. "Tell your parents I'll call them in the morning."

"They still think we're together," Franco said. "And they think it's strange you haven't come around."

Sofia raised her hands. "Why do they think that?"

Franco narrowed his eyes. "For the same reason your parents still think we're together."

Sofia's stomach dropped. She couldn't even call it a low blow since it was the truth.

"Just come with me," Franco pleaded. "For an hour or two."

When she didn't answer, he changed tactics.

"I'm sorry for intruding on whatever you've got going on here." He waved his arms about. "But I'm on the spot, and I'm asking you for help. I did the same for you."

Sofia wanted to point out that on the one day he was

supposed to show up for her, he'd managed to get himself arrested. But the door swung open again, and Jon had murder in his eyes. Desperate to keep the two men apart, she grabbed Jon by the arm and led him back into the house, slamming the door shut behind them.

"Here's the thing," she said, speaking very fast. "I've got to go with him for an hour or two."

Anger flashed in Jon's eyes. "You're not leaving here with him."

"Yes, I am."

This was the wrong day for him to test her. She was going to do this last thing and that was all there was to it. She couldn't have Franco out there, thinking she owed him, stopping by every so often with a special request.

"Sofia—"

"Trust me, Jon," she said. "I have to do this one thing. I'll be back in time for dinner, and we'll talk about it."

"In time for dinner?" He let out a dry laugh. "Listen, leave here with him and—"

"And what?"

He didn't have to finish his sentence for the threat to have its full effect. For a long painful moment, they stared at each other. This wasn't a negotiation. This was a battle and Sofia would not let him win.

"Shit!" he murmured under his breath. He grabbed his keys off a hook and headed toward the garage.

"Jon, don't do this!" Sofia cried, before her pride could stop her.

She heard the garage door open and the Porsche engine fire up to life.

For two nerve-racking hours, Sofia tried to reassure Franco's parents, Valentina and Ralph, the most loveable future in-laws any woman could hope to have, on subjects she had little to no knowledge of. She told them that Franco hadn't broken any laws and his name would be cleared in due time. She told them their son was a good citizen who had always paid his taxes. She told them there was nothing to worry about. She even agreed to join them for dinner the following evening to celebrate Valentina's birthday. Then she got up and left. It felt wrong to be back in the condo she and Franco had shared. And she figured enough time had passed for Jon to calm down. He was the only one she wanted to talk to.

He wasn't there when she got back. Sofia tried calling him and heard his iPhone ringing on the kitchen counter where he'd left it. Disheartened, Sofia reasoned that he had to come back soon. The man couldn't live without his phone.

Outside, the sun was setting. The skinny palm trees in the far end of the yard cast long sinewy shadows over the pool.

Leave here with him and—

And what? Anxiety bubbled up inside her. Here she sat, waiting for him to come home and make everything sweet again. Take her out for tapas. Make her laugh. Make love to her. But Jon had the power to crush as well as to restore. He had *all* the power. She'd come so far. Was it only to wait for yet another man to live up to her expectations?

What exactly was she doing?

Chapter 21

There was a price to pay for choking. When Jon returned to an empty house late Sunday night, he learned that lesson. At the party, he'd had the opportunity to tell Sofia he loved her and he'd choked, for lack of a better word. With her ex standing at his door, the time hadn't seemed right. But maybe if he had said it, instead of threatening her like a jackass, she wouldn't have left, taking everything, her few clothes and even the goddamn fish.

The truth was, Jon didn't have the language for love. He could count on his killer communication skills to succeed professionally. He was an ace at negotiations and no one could deliver a closing argument like him. When he wasn't working, he could talk trash with the best of them. But he couldn't recall the last time—in his adult life, anyway—he'd told a single person he loved them. It just didn't come up in everyday conversation.

After he stormed out of the house, leaving Sofia and Franco alone together, he'd spent his evening at the office, trying to put a dent in the work that had piled up during his trip to Jersey. Every time he'd thought of calling her, he couldn't shovel enough pride out of the way to do it. Thus, giving her ample time to pack up and leave without even a courtesy goodbye letter.

In his defense, Sofia was in the wrong. He'd put up with a lot, but this was a bridge too damn far. To have that man show up at their door, interrupting their day and for her to leave with him. The worst was that she'd expected Jon to understand. What kind of mess was that? He was angry and had every right to be.

Anger, however, made a poor companion. It abandoned him the moment he fell onto the bed, the big empty bed, and closed his eyes. Silence folded around him and filled the hollow spaces of his heart. The price to pay for choking was too high.

"Morning, boss!" Alex greeted him when he stepped out of the elevator. "You've got a staff meeting at ten."

Jon grunted something and shut himself in his office. Then he came back out and asked Alex to hunt Stephanie down.

Stephanie had new information. It wasn't good. "Turns out Ramirez had a rainy day fund he'd forgotten to report."

Jon swore under his breath. It was as if the guy was trying to look as guilty as possible.

"It's not much," Stephanie said, alarmed. "Ten grand. But it does look like—"

"Money he pocketed from his business partner's side hustle," Jon said, finishing Stephanie's thought.

"He swears that it's money he inherited from his grandfather in Puerto Rico," she said. "I'm waiting to hear back from the lawyer in San Juan who handled the transaction."

Jon was so sick of waiting. He wanted this thing handled.

"I have some good news," Stephanie said. "The prosecutor is Andrew Fordham. A little birdy tells me he's a pal of yours. Think you could reach out to him to work out a deal?"

"In exchange for what?"

"Testimony."

Jon raised his brows. "So he does know a little something about the business. Here I thought his head was up his—"

"I'll work with him," Stephanie said. "Will you reach out to Fordham? I hear he's a real hothead."

"Count on it."

Jon wasn't as confident as he sounded. Drew was a little hotheaded, and there was nothing he loved more than a conviction.

"Thanks," Stephanie said. "I'd like to wrap this up."

So would Jon. Franco wasn't as dumb as he liked to think. He'd seen the way the guy worked Sofia and had a better understanding of their dynamics. Sofia was the stronger one of the two, and Franco both resented and relied on that strength. He needed her now that his life was falling apart. When life had been good, he'd lied to her and collected naked pics from random women. This was going to end now.

Alex peeked his head into his office at noon.

"Heading out to lunch?" Jon asked, his eyes on the computer screen.

"Uh… Heading out to take the bar exam," Alex replied. "Thought I'd remind you."

Jon snapped to attention. "Is that now?"

"Friday is my last day. Taking time off to study."

"Kid, your timing!"

"I don't schedule these dumb tests." Venturing closer to the desk, he asked, "Are you all right?"

"I've got a lot going on," Jon replied.

"True," Alex conceded. "But you haven't been yourself lately. Everyone is saying that."

Jon shifted in his chair. "Everyone who? What are they saying?"

"You hit on a client's girl," Alex said. "Everyone is saying that."

"You mean Sofia?"

Alex nodded. "You made her tea and everything."

That did it. Jon raised himself slightly from his chair and pounded the desktop. Through clenched teeth, he growled, "Sofia is *mine!*"

Alex's face fell. He apologized and scurried out of the office. Jon fell back into his chair as the weight of his rage crashed down on him. Had he really flashed his teeth at the kid? He willed himself to calm down. Once his hands had steadied, he got up and walked out to Alex's workstation. He was at his desk, working at a frantic pace. When he saw Jon, he apologized again.

"I don't know what I was thinking," he said. "I crossed a line."

"Walk with me," Jon said.

They took the elevator to the twentieth floor terrace with a prime view of all of downtown, the river and Brickell. Jon leaned over the rail and hung his head. He hadn't heard from Sofia in twenty-four hours—not one word, not an angry emoji-filled text message or a go-screw-yourself email. The idea of having to return to that big empty house, of spending another night alone in that bed, was getting to him. He'd admit to anything, apologize for whatever, to avoid that.

Alex pulled out what looked like a stylus from his pocket and asked whether Jon minded.

"Mind what?" Jon asked.

"Do you mind if I vape," Alex said.

"Let me see that," Jon said.

Alex handed over the stylus and Jon tossed it over the rail, sending it falling twenty floors down into a patch of shrubs below.

Alex blinked helplessly. "I guess I deserved that."

"I'm doing you a favor," Jon said. "Quit messing with your body. You've got too much going on."

Alex grabbed onto the balcony rail as if he didn't know what to do with his hands.

"First, you've got to crush the bar exam," Jon continued. "Still planning on joining the Miami PD's office?"

"That's the plan," Alex said.

As far as plans went, it was a solid one. The kid could sharpen his litigation skills. "Then I want you to join my gym."

Alex shook his head and said he'd stick with LA Fitness. "Do you know how much PDs make? I can't afford your gym."

"First two years are on me. Graduation present."

The kid looked as if he might cry. Jon couldn't let that happen. "Now that you're sorted out, who's going to handle *my* business? Any clue?"

He'd left it up to HR to replace Alex. He hadn't wanted to go through the trouble of interviewing candidates.

"Katherine Henry," Alex said. "She's a paralegal straight out of FAMU. Used to work with Bill before he retired. Thinking about law school."

"I'll get her to think harder," Jon said. "When will I meet her?"

"How about later today?" Alex proposed. "I could have her come by. We could talk about the transition."

Jon nodded and went back to his solemn contemplation of the river.

"She's a lucky girl," Alex said.

"Katherine Henry?"

"Ms. Silva."

"She's not a girl," Jon said.

"She's a lucky woman," Alex corrected himself.

"She doesn't think so."

"Really?" Alex sounded genuinely surprised. "She'll come around. You're a great guy."

Was the kid trying to make him cry? Jon slapped him on the back. "Time to get back to work."

"You go back to work," Alex said, losing his sentimentality. "I'm on lunch break."

By 5:00 p.m., Jon couldn't take it anymore. He called Sofia. Her cell phone went straight to voice mail, so he tried her office. A cheerful voice greeted him.

"Thank you for calling Pop Miami Event Planning. This is Melissa. How may I help you?"

After he asked to speak with Sofia, he was placed on hold. Or so he thought.

There was a clicking sound and a short silence during which Jon's throat went dry, but then Melissa's voice came through loud and clear.

"Did Sofia leave early today?" she asked.

"Yes," a woman replied. "She's meeting Franco and his parents for dinner."

"It's only five. Where's this dinner? Palm Beach?"

"By their place in Aventura. Novecento. Have you ever been?"

"Yeah! The one in Brickell."

Jon picked up a pencil and jotted down the name and location of the restaurant. Then he snapped the pencil in two. *Their place?*

"Is the caller still on hold?" the other woman asked.

There was another clicking sound. "Sorry, sir. She's not in right now. Would you like to leave a message?"

"I'll try again tomorrow. Thanks."

Jon hung up and called Novecento. "Franco Ramirez calling to confirm an eight-thirty reservation."

After a long crackling pause, he got his answer. "You mean six-thirty, don't you? A reservation for four?"

An early-bird special, Jon thought viciously. Just lovely. Sofia had promised to be back before dinner, and tonight she was meeting with her fiancé's parents for dinner. Just yesterday, they'd been...happy. She'd been happy with him, at *their* place. He couldn't understand it. Sofia loved him. He knew it. Where was the woman who'd hopped on a plane, followed him to Jersey and helped defuse an extremely tense situation with a smile and a boatload of Italian food?

Jon was ready to head out to Aventura when Alex showed up at his door. Behind him was a thin young woman with large brown eyes, dark chocolate skin and long thin braids swept to one side. She looked terrified.

"Is this a good time?" Alex asked. "I have Katherine with me."

"Kathy," she said.

Jon looked to Alex, then Kathy and came up with a plan.

"How about we talk over dinner?" he proposed. "Would that make it less painful?"

"Works for me!" Alex said.

Kathy brightened up. "I'll grab my purse!"

"Good." Jon said. "I know just the place."

The waiter filled their glasses with water. "Today's special is the gaucho steak paired with an excellent Cabernet from Spain."

Alex ordered a Heineken. Kathy looked up from her menu and said, "Just water for me."

"Are you sure about that water?" Jon asked.

"Last call for alcohol," Alex teased.

"Okay," she said, clearly relieved. "I'll try the Mojito Novecento."

Jon finalized the order. "And I'll have that Cab."

"Excellent, sir."

The Argentinian bistro was all red and gold and dark polished wood. Jon had picked a table near the restaurant's entrance for better visibility. It was six-thirty on the dot. The waiter returned with their drinks.

Alex attempted to lead what should have been a professional business dinner. "Should we start with the caseload?"

Kathy looked past Alex and out the window to the outdoor patio. "I may be imagining this," she said. "But there's a woman outside staring at us…as if we owe her money."

Alex jerked around to see. But a calm that had eluded Jon up until that point finally settled in. He picked up his glass, gave the velvety red wine a swirl, and counted to ten. By the time he reached eight, Sofia zipped past their table making a beeline for the restrooms. Her profile was partially masked by all that hair, but the tension in her clenched jaw was obvious—at least to Jon.

Alex made a clumsy attempt to distract Kathy. "Thinking about going with the burger. What looks good to you?"

"I don't know. Maybe the sliders?"

Jon put down his glass and excused himself. "Order whatever you like, and the gaucho steak for me. Medium rare. I'll be right back."

Chapter 22

Sofia stepped out of the ladies' room and found Jon waiting out in the hall. She had fully expected him to be there and still she froze. The night spent at Miguel's and the long empty hours at the office had gutted her. Having to sit with Franco and his parents, smiling while he held her hand, was absolute torture. Then to look up and spot Jon at a table inside the restaurant, looking casual as if his very presence wasn't a hostile act—*that* finally did her in.

"What are you doing here?" she demanded.

A waiter brushed past them and pushed through the double doors leading to the kitchen.

He shrugged. "Staff meeting."

"Bullshit. How did you know where to find me?"

"Maybe teach *your* staff how to use a mute button."

Damn it! The phone in the reception area had been acting iffy all week, and she'd ignored Melissa's complaints.

Her waiter swept past on his way to the kitchen. Sofia flagged him down. "Could you bring us a slice of cake with a candle when we order coffee later?"

"No cake this afternoon. Is a brownie okay?"

"Sure. Whatever."

"Ever the event planner," Jon said. "What are you celebrating?"

"Franco's mother's birthday."

"Should I send over champagne?"

"Whatever you send over, I'll send back."

"So touchy when it comes to your in-laws," he said.

"This is just for appearances, Jon," Sofia said. "And they're good people. I don't want to hurt their feelings."

"But you're okay hurting mine."

Sofia was speechless. The playfulness of his manner had turned, and she didn't know how to respond. Another waiter walked past them, and she said the first thing that came to mind. "You left and never came back. We had dinner plans."

Jon took a step forward. When he moved like that, light and quick, she was all the more aware of his size. Now they were close enough to kiss. The creases at the corners of his eyes ran deep. He looked as drained as she felt.

"Let's get this straight," he said. "You left because I was late for dinner?"

"No," Sofia said. "I left because you gave me an ultimatum. Remember?"

"Technically, I didn't," he said. "You didn't give me the chance. And even if I had, it would've been justified considering the circumstances."

"Circumstances that I tried to explain to you," Sofia said. "If you really think I wanted to leave with him, then you don't know me, Jon Gunther."

A woman came around the corner and stopped abruptly. She eyed Sofia and Jon blocking the way to the restrooms. Jon grabbed her hand and pulled her through the swinging doors into the kitchen. Then, unexpectedly, he kissed her, proving that he did know her a little bit. Anger turned to flaming passion. Sofia grabbed his jacket lapel and kissed him hard. When he pulled away, she pressed her swollen lips together, savoring the kiss.

"What am I tasting?" he whispered.

"What are you talking about?" she whispered back.

"What are you drinking?" he asked.

She crinkled her nose. "White Zinfandel."

"Didn't the waiter tell you about the Cab from Spain?" he asked. "It's amazing."

Was he questioning her taste in wine now? "The Cab would go to my head. Zinfandel is a safe bet for dinner with future in-laws."

"Future what?" he asked.

"*Former* in-laws," she corrected. "Kiss me again before I go back out there."

He shook his head no, all the while doing her the service of wiping her smudged lipstick with the pad of his thumb. "You go back out there and drink Zinfandel."

The chef approached. "As much as you two are making me swoon," she said, wiping her hands on a white towel. "I need you to get out."

Sofia raised a hand and pleaded, "Just a minute!"

She was determined to set him straight. The kiss didn't mean capitulation. It meant he was a good kisser, that's all.

"Asking for *a minute* doesn't work for everything, Sofia," Jon said cuttingly. "Sometimes it makes things worse."

Okay—that was a low freaking blow! A *minute* ago, he'd had his tongue down her throat. He took her left hand in his and pointed out the diamond on her fourth finger.

"It doesn't mean anything," she said.

"You say that a lot," he said.

"Jon…"

"Go. Your future in-laws are waiting."

"Former! Former in-laws!"

"You tell them that."

The chef snapped her towel. "Both of you! Out!"

Sofia was in a mood when she got back to the table. Franco explained that they'd waited for her to start their meal, but the food was getting cold.

"I had to take a call," she said. "Sorry. It was rude of me."

Franco's mother patted her hand and said she worked too hard. When Franco tried to hold that same hand, Sofia pulled it away and flagged the waiter. She exchanged her glass of Zinfandel for the Cabernet.

The conversation picked up again. Franco was giving his father an update. He said his *accountant* had forgotten to report the money he'd inherited from his grandfather. "That's all it is," he said. "I may have to pay a fine and back taxes. But for sure I'll fire the accountant."

Franco laughed at his own little joke. Sofia couldn't laugh. Franco's story had changed so many times it was hard to keep up. What was this about an inheritance? This was the first she'd heard of it. And here she'd thought he was cash poor.

After dinner, her sorry quartet walked past Jon's table. They looked as if they were having fun, laughing and chatting happily. Sofia couldn't help stealing a glance at him. Jon winked. She turned away, her cheeks hot.

They dropped Franco's parents off at his cousin's house in Pembroke Pines. Then they drove back to Miami in painful silence. Franco pulled up to Miguel's building and parked in a visitor's spot. Sofia reached for the door handle. He stopped her, trying once again to grab hold of her hand. This time, Sofia objected.

"Stop doing that!" she cried.

"I can't even touch you?" Franco sounded hurt. "We can't have dinner without your boyfriend showing up? Think I didn't notice?"

Sofia dug her nails into the palm of her hands, praying for restraint. How could she make him understand? He had shown up and disrupted their lives, not the other way around.

"Sofia, I'm going through a lot right now. I could use a friend."

"We can't be friends," she said. "You lied to me. I've lied to everyone. All we've done is spread deception and I'm sick of it."

Those lies, like so many stones, were piling up, sealing the cave and trapping them both in the past. Sofia wanted out.

"Since we're talking about lying, I wasn't totally honest with my folks at dinner today," he said. "It's not as simple as I made it sound."

No kidding!

"There's a chance I can work out a deal with the prosecutors, but I'm leaving Pike high and dry."

"What does Steve Pike have to do with this?" Sofia asked.

Franco only shook his head, which was fine with Sofia because, on second thought, she didn't want to know.

"If he got you into this, then he wasn't looking out for you," she said. "Save your business."

"The thing is, it was more his business than mine," Franco said. "It always was."

"What are you saying now? You two are partners."

"I might've exaggerated my role in the company."

Sofia recoiled. *Who was this man?*

"Why, Franco?" she asked.

"To impress you."

Bullshit. He wasn't going to pin this on her.

"It's true. You were a kickass business owner, and I was a car salesman."

"I'm sorry you felt that way," Sofia said, unconvinced. Deep down she knew that he'd lied because it was easy for him. In comparison, Jon's blunt honesty was refreshing.

"If you can't save the business, save your reputation. Free yourself and get on with your life."

"Is that what you're doing?" he asked bitterly. "Getting on with your life."

"I'm trying to."

"Are you with him to get back at me?" he asked.

"I'm not interested in getting back at you," she said. "I only want to get back to him. You've taken up too much of my time already."

"What do you see in him? I get he's a lawyer, and some women may like that type, but...you, Sofia?"

Sofia was done. She pushed the door open and stepped out of the car. Whatever type Jon was, yes, absolutely, she liked it.

"Don't go," Franco said. "Can't you give me a minute?"

"No." Sometimes a minute only made things worse. But for the sake of their shared history, she left him with some advice. "Do what you've got to do to get your life back on track. Then make some new friends."

She left him in the parking lot, trusting that he knew his way out, and rode the elevator to Miguel's place to freshen up. She had a plan. She figured Jon would head back to the office after dinner with his staff. She'd go there and demand they talk. His office was the perfect neutral setting. It was intimate enough for frank conversation. And, if they locked the door, it was perfect for anything else they might want to do.

She figured she had time to change out of her beige dress and into something more colorful. Jon loved her in color. She might as well use every tactical advantage she had. Plus, she had to lose the ring.

Sofia was rummaging through her cramped closet when Leila called.

"Good news!" Leila exclaimed. "The Star Island open house was a hit. We've got a bidding war going on. Once we close, I'm buying a new car. A hot one."

"Can I double my fee, then?" Sofia yanked a hanger free, examined the blue-and-white striped dress and rejected it. "I could use the money. I need a bigger closet—and a place of my own."

Sofia bent down and carefully removed a Stuart Weitzman shoebox from a precarious shoebox tower, Jenga-style.

"Now you're talking," Leila said. Her tone had changed from light and cheery to straight up serious. "Come by the office and we'll go over your options."

"I will," Sofia said. "Just not now. I'm on a mission."

"A Jon Gunther mission?" Leila asked. She was light and cheery again.

Sofia sank to the floor and fastened the tiny buckles of a strappy sandal with a sharp heel. While she was at it, she got Leila up to speed.

"Let's recap," Leila said. "He caught you having dinner with your ex and ex in-laws?"

"He didn't *catch* me," Sofia said. "He tracked me down. It's not the same."

"Why is Franco still in the picture?"

"He's not!"

"Are we looking at the same picture?" Leila asked. "Because if I told Nick I had to go off with my ex for a cozy family reunion…I'd like to think he'd be understanding, but I think he'd lose his mind."

"This isn't about Nick!" Sofia cried, but only because she didn't know what else to say. Leila was right. What if *Viv* had shown up at their door? How would she have handled it? She'd put Jon in an untenable position. Up until

Sunday, he'd handled it with grace. But everyone had a tipping point.

Another call came through. It was Nick.

"Hold on, Leila."

Sofia switched lines. Nick got straight to the point. "It's going down next Friday. Renovations are done. The house will be furnished and ready."

"Oh, gosh…"

Sofia lay flat on the carpeted floor. Did Nick and Leila exist solely to show her how good love could be? Maybe instead of arguing with Leila, she should listen to her. Obviously, she knew a thing or two.

"You'll help set up?" Nick asked.

"Leave it to me."

"You have a blank check," he said. "Only no fireworks. Keep it simple."

Was he worried she'd show up with a marching band? "It'll be tasteful. I promise."

Leila was more subdued when Sofia got back on the line. "You're going through a lot. I shouldn't have piled it on."

"I needed to hear it." Sofia sat cross-legged on the floor. "What do I do now, genius?"

"You want my advice?"

"Lay it on me."

"For starters," Leila said. "There's nothing a little bit of lingerie can't fix."

It turned out Leila knew nothing at all. When she opened her white trench coat to reveal a delicate blue lace bodysuit, Jon was not affected. He got up from behind his desk in what looked to be a promising move, but then adjusted the lapel of her coat and fastened the buttons.

"You said you're here to talk," he said.

"I am." She assumed they'd talk after he shoved all the

files off his desk and took her on the glossy wood surface—like in every movie!

He tied the belt in a solid knot. "Then I'll need a clear head."

"I'm trying to make amends," Sofia said. "I shouldn't have left the way I did, without a word of explanation. That was wrong. But you shouldn't have—"

"No," he said. "You don't get to do that."

"What?" she asked.

"Tell me what my position ought to be."

He leaned back onto the desktop and folded his arms across his chest. His blazer had been tossed onto the couch with neglect. His gunmetal gray tie was loose. He looked devilishly undone and, to her mind, had every advantage she might have had in lingerie.

"Okay. I'll speak for myself," Sofia said. "Franco's parents were freaking out about his legal troubles. He asked me to help reassure them. I wore the ring. I did my part."

"Why is it your job to reassure them?" Jon asked.

"It's not," she admitted. "I owed Franco a favor."

"How do you figure?"

"He kept our breakup secret when it was convenient for me."

"So, what?" Jon asked. "On Sunday he came to collect?"

"You could say that," Sofia replied.

"What do you say?" Jon asked.

"I didn't want him thinking he could show up whenever he liked, asking for favors," Sofia said. "I wanted to settle the score."

"I'd believe you if I hadn't seen you with his parents," Jon said. "You care for them."

"What if I do, Jon?" Sofia asked. "I've known them for years. Would that be so wrong?"

"Yes, if he can use them to get to you."

"Maybe you don't understand because you don't know how families work," she said. "Or what it feels like to be tied to one. How your failures can let everybody down."

She didn't know if she was talking about Franco's family or her own. Everything was one big mess in her mind.

"Here's the thing," he said. "I don't believe for a minute you're doing any of this for his family or yours."

"You think I still have feelings for him?" Sofia asked, incredulous.

"You left me because of him."

"I left you because of you!"

Sofia was so in love with him, she was drowning in it. She needed to know if he felt the same. The last woman who'd assumed she had a future with Jon had had a rude awakening.

"Jon, I can't play house with you forever."

"Is that what you think we were doing? Playing?"

"I have no clue," she said. "So, now would be a good time to tell me how you feel."

"How I feel is not the issue."

"What's the issue?"

"Your secrets."

"Don't exaggerate," she said. "I chose not to go public with a very private matter until the time was right. That's all."

"When will the time be right?"

"Saturday."

"Why Saturday?"

Sofia explained that her parents were back at work after their European vacation and physically exhausted. "I'll stop by their house on Saturday and we'll talk."

Even as she said this, Sofia knew how it sounded. She was making excuses, postponing something that should have been handled months ago.

"Then we'll table this discussion until Sunday."

"Are you serious?" she asked. There was no need to draw a line in the sand.

"Sofia," he said. "I want you free and clear of encumbrances."

Free and clear of what?

"Is this the only way you can talk? With a bunch of legal jargon?"

Suddenly, the legal talk wasn't sexy anymore. She'd hate to be up against Jon in a legal matter, if this was how he handled matters of the heart.

"It is when I'm dead serious."

"Jon, you have me."

"Do you still have his ring?"

Sofia flushed with embarrassment. "Forget the ring. At this point, it's just a prop."

"A prop you never hesitated to use against me."

Sofia lowered her eyes, silenced. For Jon, the little diamond was a boulder blocking the way forward. It truly was kryptonite.

Jon walked around her and opened his office door. "And you remembered enough to take it off before coming here."

"Wait. Are you kicking me out?" she asked. "I'd think twice before you do."

If Jon was bothered, panicked or worried in any way, it didn't show. "I'm ending this before it goes too far," he said. "You know my conditions."

"Conditions?" she said. "Do you hear yourself? Real love is unconditional."

He wasn't moved. "For better men, maybe. Not me."

Sofia wanted to slap that smug look off his face.

"And what do I get out of this?" she asked. "A man who doesn't know what it means to belong to anything except this stupid law firm?"

The smug look was replaced with something darker. She could feel him retreating and locking doors so she could never get to him.

This had officially gone too far.

Jon was so proud of his work. His professional accomplishments had made him the man that he was: successful, confident and independent. He was free and able to deal with his family on his own terms. She, on the other hand, was taking her cues not only from her parents but her former in-laws, as well.

"Jon, I didn't mean that."

He didn't answer. And when the silence became unbearable, Sofia walked out the open door. She marched past the empty cubicles, heading toward the elevators, her pride keeping her upright.

"Sofia," he called out.

She turned around, hopeful. "Yes?"

"You know damn well what you get when you get me, and it's worth the work."

Chapter 23

Leila stirred artificial sweetener into her green tea. "You're young and single—more or less. You want to be in a cool building. Up your chance to meet someone interesting at the pool or the gym."

Sofia nodded and stared out the window. It was a gloomy day. All the surrounding buildings were shrouded in fog. Sofia was alone with Leila in the conference room with a tray of rainbow-hued macarons between them. Of all the times she'd stopped by the agency, this was the first time she'd been given the royal treatment, which included her choice of coffee, tea or champagne. The difference: she was a client.

Disheartened, Sofia pushed away her teacup. She liked her tea the way Jon made it for her—dark and rich with milk and real sugar. And she had no interest in meeting anyone new, interesting or not, at the pool, the gym or anywhere else. But as Leila had said, she was more or less single. She hadn't heard from Jon since he'd slapped her with an ultimatum. For a day or so, she'd found strength in her wounded pride. Then a day or two passed, the weather changed and Sofia's mood changed with it. June had brought constant rainstorms. The gloom that had taken over the skies had settled in her heart. By the end of the week, she'd begun to suspect the mysterious forces that had brought them together through a string of chance meetings were not strong enough to keep them together.

Then her mother had called to remind her about Father's Day. It was coming up in a couple of weeks and she'd made reservations at her dad's favorite restaurant. Her dad never wanted gifts for the occasion, but a family dinner was mandatory.

"Remember to tell Franco," her mom said. "Remind him that he is always welcome in our family."

Her mother assumed that Franco had been avoiding the family out of shame over his legal troubles—as if Franco had any shame. Sofia said only that she'd be stopping by on Saturday afternoon and hung up.

Saturday it would all be over. She had no intention of messing up her timeline to meet Jon Gunther's demands.

Leila reached out and touched her shoulder. "I know it's overwhelming," she said. "We don't have to move so fast."

Actually, they weren't moving fast enough. "I need someplace to live."

"Then I recommend you rent," Leila said. "I have clients who own investment properties. I'll hook you up with a high-end condo with all the amenities."

Nick poked his head through the conference room door. Sofia watched a man known for his charm and confidence go wooden. "Hey! Um… How are you, Sofia? How are things shaping up?"

Leila let out a nervous laugh. "What kind of question is that?"

It was a question that Sofia understood. "Everything is shaping up great."

When she wasn't working, Sofia was cooped up in her bedroom at Miguel's, drafting the final touches for the wedding proposal. Leila might not be into fireworks, but who didn't love flowers? Sofia planned to turn their new home into an enchanted garden.

"Okay," Nick said. "Good seeing you."

Leila apologized for his odd behavior. "I'm not crazy. Something is up with that man. Do you think he's nervous about moving into the new house? It's a big step for us."

It was a big step for any couple! No matter how happy you were with someone, how much in love, you had to use your head when planning a future. You couldn't just move in, cross your fingers, and hope for the best.

But no, she didn't think Nick was nervous about it, not in the slightest.

"You lucked out with Nick," Sofia replied. "He's a great guy."

"True. Whenever I showed up at his place half-naked, he had the decency to seal the deal," Leila joked.

The joke brought back the bittersweet memory. Sofia turned to the windows again. The fog had thickened. It was going to rain.

"Sofia, don't cry!" Leila cried.

Was she crying? She touched her cheek and sure enough, it was wet. She took a napkin off the tray and dabbed her eyes.

Leila circled the table and sat next to her. "How did you leave things with Jon?"

Sofia didn't reply. How to explain they'd retreated to their respective camps to refuel and recharge? Such were the rules of engagement. Jon's "conditions" weren't unreasonable, but the way he'd made them absolutely was. And she would not back down.

Faced with her silence, Leila continued. "When Jon told me he wanted to buy the house, I tried to talk him out of it. I wasn't sure it was the house for him. I was still trying to find him the perfect bachelor pad."

Sofia blew her nose. "He wanted a home."

"You're the only one who knew that." Leila took a deep breath before speaking again. "The way he insisted on keeping the furniture, all of it, even the patio furniture... why do you think?"

"It was convenient."

Jon was busy. He didn't have time to pick out coffee tables and area rugs.

"You know what would've been more convenient?" Leila asked. "A furnished condo in one of the buildings I plan to show you."

Sofia rejected Leila's theory. The house was perfect, better than any furnished condo. And anyway, what was she hinting at?

"You don't think he bought the house for me. Right?"

"I think he bought it with you in mind," Leila said. "Maybe he had a feeling. The first time I saw you two together, I had a feeling."

Sofia had had a whole range of feelings, and now those feelings were all in a knot in her chest.

Leila handed her a vibrant royal blue *macaron* that stained her tongue. She left the agency feeling as blue as ever.

Nick was pacing the front yard when Sofia pulled up to the house on Friday evening. The secluded neighborhood sat on an island off the main road, and the moment Sofia drove through the guard gate, she'd felt instant calm. This was her first visit to the house since the renovation. She'd expected high glam and wasn't disappointed. The house had a stripped-down Miami feel. The main living area sparkled with light pouring in from the second floor skylight. Its sweeping space was made intimate by sheer cream curtain panels accentuating the double-height windows. The furniture was chic and understated. Sofia admired the butter leather couches and exotic wood tables in the living area. French doors opened to the yard, pool and the dock beyond. Everything spoke of easy living and peace. It was no wonder Leila couldn't shut up about it.

Sofia put Nick in charge of lighting the dozens of candles that he'd insisted on floating in the pool. When he was done, sweating and smelling of butane, he assured her it was worth it. "She did this at our first open house. The pool was smaller, less candles."

"I remember," Sofia said.

She sent him off to shower. Nick hesitated and asked if she was holding up okay. "Was it selfish of me to ask you to do this?"

"Don't be dumb. This is the one thing I've been looking forward to," Sofia said. "I'm happy to help."

He left her to finish up. Minutes later, the florist arrived with a truckload of white roses and orchids. Having had to conceive of the design for the space based only on the photos Leila had shared, Sofia had played it safe. She'd picked plain crystal hurricane vases to hold candles and flowers alike. After a few tries with different patterns, she lined the vases along a path of white organza from the front door to the patio, allowing the fabric to spill down the large steps to the pool. The candlelight drew blue shadows from the crystal. And now that the sun had set, the pool glowed as if on fire. Magic.

Nick returned to inspect her work after the florist had packed up and left. Sofia held her breath, anxious for his approval. He stood out on the patio with his back to her, hands in pockets. Time passed and he said nothing.

She knew she'd done her job.

She patted Nick on the back. "Good luck."

Sofia was packing up her things when she heard footsteps at the door and keys rattling. Panic struck through her. She scurried back outside, searching for Nick.

"She's here! She's here!"

Nick consulted his watch. "She's not due until—"

The door creaked open.

Nick snapped into action, grabbed Sofia by the shoulders and guided her into the kitchen. "Stay here until I can take her out back."

Sofia didn't want to stay, but since she had no choice she helped herself to a chocolate-covered strawberry from the silver tray she'd set out and hunched low behind the kitchen island. From her hiding place, she didn't hear much, just a gasp and a sigh.

Nick's voice was shredded. "Love, you're trembling."

Sofia was trembling, too. As soon as the French doors clicked shut behind them, she scrambled to the kitchen window. There they were surrounded by flowers and bathed in candlelight. Leila's face was buried in Nick's chest. He was holding her, stroking her back. Sofia didn't have the heart of a voyeur. She wiped her own tears and tiptoed to the door.

On her way to her parents' house late Saturday afternoon, Sofia rehearsed her speech. She figured if her mother's heart was strong enough to handle a three-week tour of Italy, it could handle the truth. She veered off Biscayne Boulevard and headed west toward the Miami Shores neighborhood where she'd grown up and her parents had lived for decades. If she'd turned east, she would have been heading toward the waterfront and the grand homes she'd admired as a kid. The west side was less grand, but more lively.

Sofia rounded a corner and spotted a silver Dodge Viper in her parents' driveway, next to her mother's Camry, and occupying the spot usually reserved for her. She instantly recognized it as belonging to Franco's fleet of loaners— the fun cars his customers got to drive when their vehicles were in the shop. She parked curbside and slammed her car door shut.

She found Franco, his parents and her own gathered in the living room. Sofia took in the scene from the front door. For the briefest moment, it looked normal and right. There they were chatting, sipping soda in her mother's oversized glasses and passing around a bowl of chips. The TV was on. Franco looked relaxed in a T-shirt and cargo shorts. He grinned at her.

The grin pushed Sofia over the edge. He had no right to be here. Everything she'd done, every lie and scheme, had been to hide the basic truth: he had hurt her. She'd refused to admit it and hadn't wanted anyone else to know it, either. It had challenged her core identity. She was the successful one, the smart one. Sofia the Badass, as she'd been called in high school. Her friends admired her and her staff looked up to her. And yet, she'd been duped and cheated on. She'd been passed over for some faceless women on a smartphone screen. Jon was right. Her mother's health and her family ties with Franco had only been an excuse. She'd wasted months doing all she could to reshape their story, write an alternative ending in which she came out ahead. It had all been a waste of time.

"Sofia!" her father called out to her. "We're celebrating the news."

"What news?"

She drew quizzical looks from both sets of parents. Her mother tried to cover for her. "You know! The charges were dropped. Franco is innocent."

Sofia shook her head. Franco was no innocent.

"Now that this…unpleasantness is behind us," her mother continued, "we can all move forward."

"I'd like that," Franco said. "How about you, Sofia?"

"I agree," Sofia said.

Sofia walked over to the couch and sat next to her father, plopped her large tote bag on her lap and started digging for the jewelry box she'd been carrying around for four months now.

"So you'll set the date?" her mother asked.

"No."

Franco's mother spoke up. "Sofia, we're leaving tomorrow. I'd like to give our friends back home a date."

Franco jumped in. "She's saying we need time to work out the details."

"No!" Sofia looked up from her task. "*I'm* saying Franco and I are not getting married."

"They've been through a lot," Franco's dad said. "It makes sense if they want to wait."

"No, that's not it," Sofia said. "Franco and I are done. We were only waiting to tell you."

Her mother let out a gasp. "Done?"

"Done."

The rapid-fire questions came from all sides. "Since when?"

"What happened?"

"Why didn't you tell us?"

While Franco stayed resolutely quiet, Sofia answered them the best she could. Only she refused to satisfy their curiosity beyond the strict facts. "What happened is between Franco and me."

Her father turned off the TV. Her mother went into the kitchen and returned with a glass of water, even though she had been drinking from one. Sofia studied her face and was satisfied that her health was holding up. Then everyone fell silent for a long while, each grappling with the truth.

The last time they were all gathered in this room, it was the night of their engagement party. Franco's mother had looked lovely. She'd spent north of two hundred dollars on her sequined dress, the most she had ever spent on a single article of clothing. The mood had been lighter, both their parents genuinely looking forward to a lifetime of friendship.

Valentina Ramirez looked at Sofia with clear disappointment. She'd always relied on her to keep Franco on track. In high school, she'd recruited Sofia to help Franco with his studies. In college, she'd begged Sofia to curb his partying. Now, as an adult, the request was to keep Franco on the good side of the law. It was too much to ask.

Her dad came to sit next her, shielding her in the way fathers protect daughters from worrisome prom dates. He patted her on the shoulder and muttered, *"Lo sabía."*

Sofia went back to digging through her purse. She found the ring box and placed it on the coffee table before Franco. They locked eyes. For the first time since their breakup, he looked genuinely sorry.

Chapter 24

On Wednesday afternoon, Jon had skipped his workout to work on Drew. He leaned against the bare concrete wall while Drew exhausted himself at the speed bag. When Drew stopped to catch a breath, he looked Jon in the eye and asked, "What's it to you, anyway?"

"Come on," Jon said. "You're not going to give me a hard time for such a small player."

"You make my point." Drew raised his gloved fists to eye level. "Why is your firm bringing out the big guns? Pun intended."

It was early and the gym had yet to fill up. From the weight room, an occasional grunt or clash of iron punctuated the relative silence. Drew resumed his steady rhythmic swings. One. Two. *I already knew how to count to two.* Jon winced. Any little thing reminded him of Sofia, each memory a sonic blow to the chest.

"Stephanie asked me to talk to you," Jon said coolly. "I'm already bored with the whole business."

"Is Stephanie single?" Drew asked.

Jon glanced at his watch. They'd been at this long enough; it was time to wrap things up. He pushed off the wall. Drew instinctively backed away, leaving the speed bag swinging aimlessly.

"I don't want to tell you how to do your job—"

"Then don't."

"You really should be jumping all over this."

"I can't let Ramirez walk free."

"You've got no evidence that he was involved in this scheme. Pike's your man."

"I've got ten grand of unreported funds," Drew said. "That's one count conspiracy, at least."

"There's no conspiracy, Drew," Jon said. "There's one idiot who didn't report some inheritance. We can trace the money back to his granddad. Don't waste your time."

"Will this idiot testify against the other idiot?"

"Gladly."

Drew returned to the bag, fists up. "Okay. Let's do it."

On Saturday, Jon was fueling up the Porsche at a gas station downtown when Leila pulled up in a brand-spanking new red Tesla. He was going to ask if she'd finally put the little Mazda to rest, but when she sprang out of the car she had other news.

"Look at this!" she cried. "I'm engaged."

She held out her left hand. Jon stared at her impressive rock for a long time. Then he leaned back against his car, light-headed. Was a ring the answer? Was that what Sofia wanted? She seemed to like being engaged, to the point of faking it. Maybe the time had come for him to step up in a major way. At this point, desperation had settled in. He'd lived alone most of his adult life and had never known this loneliness. He needed to make things right with Sofia. He'd try anything.

"This is when you say congratulations," Leila said.

He apologized and gave her a hug. "Congratulations! Nick is a lucky guy."

"You should've seen how nervous he was," Leila said. "He'd been planning it for weeks."

She went on to describe the proposal in some detail. Jon stayed focused on the ring. It was nothing like the

Cracker Jack ring Franco had given Sofia. Still, he knew he could top it.

"Isn't that sweet?" Leila asked.

He had no idea what she was talking about. He had, however, come to a decision. "Leila, where can I get one of those?"

"One what?" she asked.

"A ring," he specified. "Where would you recommend I get one?"

She brought her left hand to her chest in a protective gesture. "Who are you buying this ring for?"

"Who do you think?" he asked.

She took a deep breath before starting over. "You want to buy a ring for Sofia? My Sofia?"

"She's *my* Sofia," Jon said. "If I'm going to propose, I'll need a ring."

He'd propose just as soon as she assured him Franco was gone for good. That was his position from which he would not waver, even if it killed him—and it was killing him. But Leila didn't need to know any of that.

"Does she know?" Leila asked.

"We're not on speaking terms," Jon said. "That'll change."

"How can you be sure?" Leila asked. "Sofia is stubborn."

"I'm sure," Jon said.

He was banking on that very stubbornness. Sofia loved him. Everything confirmed it: the way she touched him, said his name, made love to him. She would not walk away from that love.

Leila gripped him by the shoulders, her nails digging through his shirt. Jon wondered if he'd made a mistake asking for her help. He wouldn't want to steal her engagement-news thunder.

"Do you know what this means, Jon?" she asked. "I'm in the loop! For once I'm in the loop!"

Was the heat getting to her? "What loop?"

"Never mind," she said. "My ring is from Tiffany. I love it. Cartier recently opened a boutique in the Design District, so that's an option."

He thought it over. "I've got cuff links from Cartier. Let's go there."

"You want to go right now?" Leila asked.

"Is that a problem?" He didn't know when Sofia would come around. When she did, he had to be ready.

Leila darted back to her car. "Follow me! Try to keep up!"

"Didn't you stop for gas?" he called after her.

"Nope! I stopped for you," she said. "Besides, this car runs on air."

Late Monday afternoon, Sofia called an impromptu staff meeting. Ericka and Melissa took the seats facing her desk, purses and tote bags packed and ready for a quick getaway. Every now and then, they stole glances at their watches or checked the time on their phones.

Sofia clasped her hands before her. "I'm planning a private event for the Fourth of July and would like some help."

"What do you have in mind?" Ericka asked.

"A picnic on the beach type of thing," Sofia said.

"But the beach will be so crowded!" Melissa cried.

"She's right," Ericka said. "Who's the client, anyway?"

"I am."

After she'd left her parents' house, all she'd wanted to do was speed over to Jon's house, climb into bed and resume their life together as if nothing had happened. But something *had* happened. For the first time in their relationship, she was free…of all encumbrances. And it felt amazing. Now she wanted only to make up for everything she'd put him through.

"Something nice for you and Franco?" Melissa asked.

"Something nice for me and…someone else."

Sofia waited for her words to make an impact. Ericka and Melissa just stared at her. Then Ericka opened her purse, thumbed through her wallet and handed Melissa a twenty. Sofia averted her eyes until the transaction was complete, but there was no escaping their taunting.

"We saw you with him at the Star Island party," Ericka said. "Our champagne-pouring hero."

"Please say it's him," Melissa implored. "I love him."

"You can't love him," Sofia said. "You don't even know him."

"I've loved him since I handed him that bottle of water," Melissa said.

"So you're thinking about a picnic?" Ericka asked.

"But catered," Sofia said. "Naturally."

Her team wasn't impressed. Ericka made a face. Melissa said she was getting a brain cramp just thinking about it.

"I'm your private event planner," Ericka said. "Why don't you leave it up to me?"

They spent the next half hour tossing about ideas. Ericka made a few calls and before they left for the evening, they had the outlines of a plan.

Once alone, Sofia reached for her old fountain pen and cardstock from her custom stationary. In her best penmanship, she wrote: Please be my guest for dining and celebration on Friday, July 4th at 6 in the evening. Coconut Grove Marina.

Then she went to deliver the invitation in person, expecting Jon to still be at his office. He wasn't.

Jon's assistant wasn't there, either. Not the guy she knew, anyway. A young woman was at his desk and her eyes widened with recognition when Sofia approached her. It took Sofia a moment to realize that she was the third person at the restaurant the night of the ambush.

"Mr. Gunther left early today," she said. "Would you like to leave a message?"

Sofia considered leaving the card, but nixed the idea. She had a few things to tell Jon beforehand. Dressed in her sharpest pencil skirt and heels, she'd come prepared to negotiate. And this time, he would hear her out.

"Do you know if he went home?" she asked. "Or out to dinner somewhere?"

"I can't share that," she said.

She typed something into the computer and turned the monitor slightly so Sofia could take a look. The screen showed the homepage of Jon's boxing gym. Sofia noted the address.

"I guess that's it then," Sofia said for the benefit of whomever Jon's assistant thought might be spying on them. "Thanks. Good night."

At the gym, there were yet more barriers to reaching Jon. Members used a key card to access what looked like an old warehouse. Sofia lingered in the entryway, feeling like a stalker. If she called Jon and asked him to meet her outside, what was the fun in that? She needed the element of surprise. After a while, a woman in a sports bra and sweatpants combo approached, swinging a pair of gloves.

"Need to get in?" she asked.

"Yes. Could you?"

"Wait." She blocked the doorway. "You're not someone's crazy ex-girlfriend, are you?"

"No!"

Sofia was outraged. The crazy ex stereotype was sexist at best, but also accurate.

"Just checking," the woman said. "We've got our share."

She waved her key card and let Sofia in.

Jon was in a ring at the center of the gym. He moved around light and quick. Sofia's belly flopped when his partner landed a jab across his jaw. His reaction was swift; swinging hard and fast, he landed two punches. *One. Two.* Sofia had never seen him like this and a jolt of excitement ran through her. Suddenly, the distance between them was too great. She rushed to the ropes and called out to him. It was likely the wrong thing to do. He turned at the sound of her voice. His partner landed another punch to his head and he toppled onto the ropes.

Sofia screamed. "Jon!" She reached up and took his face in her hands. "Oh, my God! Are you okay?"

"What the heck melodrama is going on here?" his partner asked.

Sofia shot him a dark look before realizing the man was only kidding, grinning from ear to ear. Jon recovered. He pulled himself upright, slipped between the ropes and jumped down to the floor.

She took a step forward, felt the heat rising from his glistening body and wanted desperately to throw herself at him. Thankfully, he saved her the indignity by grabbing her and kissing her passionately. His gloved hands were clumsy, but her hands were free. She gripped his arms, feeling the taut muscles. When he tried to release her, she wouldn't have it. She clung to him and kissed him harder. She had missed him so damn much.

Finally, they broke apart. The gym erupted in applause and hollers. Someone called out to Jon. "Bro, take that outside!"

Jon shielded her from it all. After he waved to their audience, he led her to the lobby and he pulled her onto a bench.

"If you're here to break up with me, I want full custody

of Little Red Fish," he said. "You didn't know he was a dude, and we've got a bromance going on."

She considered this. "He does look a little sad."

"He wants to come home," Jon said.

"You call it his home and yet if he does one thing to upset you, you'll deliver an ultimatum, maybe threaten to kick him out."

Jon looked at her for a long moment. "I would never do that."

"Little Red Fish won't be moving back in," she affirmed. "He's in the market for a condo."

Jon slipped off and dropped his gloves to the concrete floor. "You *are* here to break up with me."

"Would I've kissed you like that?" she asked.

"I'd like to think so," he replied.

Sofia twisted to face him. "I'm here with some conditions of my own."

He cocked his head, interested. "I'm listening."

She cleared her throat. "I know what I get when I get you, but you need to up your game, Jon Gunther."

He got comfortable, stretching out his long strong brown legs. "Up my game? Explain."

"The first time you called me sweetheart, I hopped on a plane to Hoboken."

"Was that it?" he asked. "I was wondering what had gotten into you."

"Jon, you say you're good with words, but when you talk to me it's all legalese. I need you to talk from the heart."

"Don't lay out your weaknesses like that," he advised. "Now I know how to get you to do anything."

"Are you listening to me?" she asked, exasperated.

Jon reached out for her hand and took her fingers to his lips. "Sofia, you hopped on a plane to Hoboken because you're bighearted and generous, and I love that about you."

Sofia's eyes glazed over and she blinked to keep from tearing up.

"Sweetheart, you've been away so long," Jon said. "Come home with me. We'll order pizza and get naked in the pool."

She had to cross her legs to contain a sudden flash of heat. Still, she managed to say, "I'm not going home with you."

"I've accepted your terms," he said. "What's the hold out?"

"If I recall, you had some conditions," Sofia said. "Aren't you going to ask if I've come through on those? Whose negotiation skills need work now?"

"I don't care anymore," he said. "We'll work it out. It's enough that you're here."

Those words, although not meant to be, were hurtful. That was the saddest thing, a fighter resigned to defeat. He didn't trust she could come through for him.

A couple of guys stumbled into the lobby to fill their water bottles from a cooler. When they were alone again, Jon whispered, "Sofia."

At the sound of her name, she closed her eyes. He reached for her and weaved his fingers into her hair. The skin on the back of her neck grew warm. She ached to be touched and kissed behind her ear, down her spine.

"Tell me you love me," he said. "That's what I want to know."

Sofia opened wide eyes and saw the turmoil in his. She lurched forward and wrapped her arms around his neck. "You *know* I do."

"Say it, then."

He'd inched his head back to better look at her. At times when emotions ran high, he never shied away.

"I love you, Jonathan Gunther-single-no kids," she said.

And the best thing? She was *free* to love him now.

He brushed back her hair. "I love you, Sofia."

Sofia closed her eyes, overwhelmed. He loved her. She'd always known it, but to hear it, to be sure, was something else.

Jon touched a finger to her jaw. "From here on out, it's you and me," he said. "We come first."

Sofia nodded. "We come first."

The heavy front door swung open and a man in a business suit walked in and made his way down a hall toward the locker room.

"I have two invitations for you," she said, and pulled out one envelope from her purse.

He opened it, read the card and raised an eyebrow. "I'm promised dinner *and* a celebration. I'm going to insist on both."

Sofia leaned in and kissed him again. "Don't worry. I'll make good on all my promises."

"And the second invitation?" he asked.

"It's for this weekend, Father's Day," Sofia said. "I'd like for you to join my family for dinner."

Chapter 25

When Jon returned to the ring, Drew had questions. "Lucky man. Who was that?"

"My future wife," Jon said. "I'll introduce you next time."

Drew raised his gloved hands. "What else are you hiding?"

A five-carat canary-yellow diamond ring in my bedroom safe, he thought. He and Drew could head out for coffee and talk about it or they could fight. Right now, Jon wanted to go a round or two.

"Come on! Move it!" he called out. "I'm feeling good."

Jon spent the rest of the week racking his brain for a gift idea for Sofia's father. Finally, Alex suggested he buy the same gift he bought his own dad, year in and year out. And at six o'clock Sunday afternoon, he pocketed the gift, checked his reflection in the bathroom mirror and set out to the restaurant on the river waterfront. As it turned out, Mr. Silva's favorite restaurant was the one Sofia had recommended on their first outing: Garcia's.

The hostess led Jon through the family-owned restaurant and he noticed for the first time the walls crammed with framed photographs going back generations. Jon felt queasy and fell out of step.

He'd managed to live a simple life by extracting himself from family ties, a trick he'd picked up from his own father. Jon had lived with his dad in Europe through his high school years. When the time came for him to set off for college, his father had declared him a "man." Which meant the only parenting he'd need going forward was the occasional phone call and pat on the back. And Jon had adapted. Sofia was glued to her family. If they were going to have any kind of future, he'd have to embrace them. They'd have to embrace him, too.

He wasn't the type of man families embraced.

"This way, sir," the hostess said.

Jon stopped short. Everything was happening so fast. From the entryway of the terrace, he saw Sofia standing at the head of a table. The others were seated. He recognized her mother and assumed the two men were her father and brother. Sofia appeared to be laying down the law, index finger stabbing the air, threatening. Her voice was hushed but it still carried. "You all better be nice!"

Sofia fighting for him… Goddamn it! It was something to see.

He had to get it together and fight for her.

Jon moved past the hostess and approached the table. Three pairs of eyes were on him. He rested a hand on Sofia's back and felt the ripples of her breath. She straightened up and leaned against him.

"Hello, everyone," he said. "I'm Jon."

Sofia's family said hello, then an awkward silence followed. Sofia invited him to sit next to her, but her father interrupted, stood and extended a hand.

"Hello, Jon," he said. "Welcome."

On Friday, July 3, Jon walked the few blocks from his office building to Clarissa Fabrics. He ducked into the doorway and a bell chimed. A sales assistant approached, asking if she could help him find a lining for a jacket or fabric for a cummerbund. Jon nodded toward Sofia's mother in the back of the store. She was assisting a woman wearing a hijab.

"I'm here to speak with Mrs. Silva," he said.

The older woman glanced his way over the rim of her glasses. She had Sofia's eyes. The assistant took over with the customer, and she shuffled over to Jon. He noted her slow, labored pace.

"Jon, what brings you here?" she asked.

He cleared his throat. "I'm here to talk to you about Sofia."

Mrs. Silva's reaction was immediate. "Why? What did she go and do now?"

"She hasn't done anything," Jon said, quick to reassure her.

"It's just that her life is so erratic lately," Mrs. Silva said wearily.

On Sunday, she'd stared at Jon from across the dining table in disapproving silence. Her demeanor hadn't softened until Jon presented Sofia's dad with premium Miami Marlins season tickets. And now, under her guarded gaze, Jon lost his nerve.

This was not how the conversation was supposed to go. He'd worn his best suit and wanted to make a good impression. But he realized the optics were wrong. He felt like a giant in the cramped store. In his dark three-piece suit, he probably looked like a bill collector or, worse, the lawyer that he was.

"It's not so erratic," Jon said. "Sofia has a good head on her shoulders."

Mrs. Silva folded her arms across her chest, much like Sofia often did. "Her friends usually don't stop by my shop, so something must be wrong."

Jon winced at the word *friend* and decided to change

tactics. No one was sending him to the friend zone. "I love your daughter. I want to marry her."

Mrs. Silva plopped down on a wooden stool behind the counter. Jon took a step forward, concerned.

She waved him away. "But you two just started dating. Am I wrong?"

From the back of the store, the sales assistant had a curiously timed coughing fit. Mrs. Silva composed herself.

"This is not the right place for this conversation," she said. "Come to the house later tonight. Whatever you have to say, you can say it to both her father and me."

Another dinner invitation… Jon took out his phone to punch in the address. "What time?"

"Seven. Do you like paella?"

Jon grinned. Yet another olive branch! "I love paella."

Ericka met with Sofia at the marina and, along with the captain of the chartered Beneteau yacht, explained what was in store. The sunset cruise would take her and Jon out on Biscayne Bay with a night sail back to the city. A catered dinner was waiting, but also Ericka had packed a cooler with champagne, oysters, caviar and ceviche. The captain assured her the spectacular night views of the downtown skyline would be even more so for the holiday.

"What do you think?" Ericka asked. "All the holiday festivities, none of the holiday crowds."

"I think it's perfect," Sofia said.

It was perfect for what she had in mind: a first date of sorts. She and Jon never had one. Theirs had been an unconventional courtship from the start. What they needed more than anything was a reboot.

Ericka checked the time. "He should be here any minute. Good luck!"

Sofia stood waiting at the marina, her heart in her throat.

It was stupid to be this nervous. They'd lived together, been on trips together and jury duty counted as a first date. Back then, at least, their hearts hadn't been on the line. They'd just been having fun. Now they wanted a full life, at least that's what she wanted.

The Porsche pulled up to the marina parking lot. She breathed in deeply, taking in the bay breeze. She was ready.

Jon was enamored with the yacht. Sofia watched as the captain gave him a guided tour. He took the wheel at the cockpit, giddy like a kid. The man she loved was gorgeous in the hazy afternoon sun. She couldn't tear her gaze away from his toasted-brown skin and dazzling smile. When he joined her on the deck, he said, "When I grow up, I want one like this."

"And you'll get it," she said. "I'm sure."

Sofia waited until they'd left the city behind before she took his hand and led him to a seat. The bay was smooth like glass. In the distance, the buildings were silhouetted against the sky. She had her little speech rehearsed and, with the sun setting in a tangerine glow, it was time.

"Jon," she said hesitantly. "I'm sorry for the way things started out with us. I wish we could wipe the slate clean."

"Don't apologize," he said. "I crowded you when you weren't ready. I could've taken a hint, given you space."

She was so glad he hadn't done those things. "I've never been as happy as when I was living with you."

"Good." He slipped off his sunglasses and looked her dead in the eyes. "Because if you buy that condo, I'm selling the house."

"What?" More conditions! Hadn't this man learned a damn thing?

"I'm serious," he said.

How could he think of selling the house? The thought

of it tore her up inside. She rose off the banquette and held on to the boat's rail to keep steady and better confront him.

"I knew the house didn't mean anything to you," she said. "It was an investment. That's all."

"It means everything to me," he said. "But I'm not going to live there without you. I'm miserable and I won't live that way."

"Where will you live?" she asked.

Was he thinking of buying a proper bachelor pad? Resuming his bachelor life?

"In the condo...with you."

"That's not the point of the condo," she said.

"What's the point of the condo?" he asked. "I've been curious."

"For us to live apart and start dating like normal people."

"That's not going to happen."

"Why not, Jon? I don't think that's too much to ask."

She must've looked like a crazy woman, curls flapping in the wild breeze and screeching like a hyena.

He stood and brushed her hair away from her face. "Because I've got a better idea."

One moment she was looking into his lively brown eyes, the next she was staring at a square-cut yellow diamond.

"What is that?" she whispered.

"What do you think?" He carefully removed the ring from its red-and-gold box. "I picked yellow because I love you in color."

He'd bought her a ring, a *gorgeous* ring, but why? Was he convinced she couldn't live without a rock on her finger? That she lived to be engaged?

"Jon, I don't need a ring," she said. "I don't need anything."

His expression darkened. "Are you saying no?"

"I'm saying it's way too soon."

"Your mother thought it was too soon," he said. "But she also thinks you're turning into a cow."

"I'm not a cow!"

"I told her as much," Jon said. "No one calls my girl a cow."

"Hold on. When did you speak with my mother?"

So much was happening; Sofia's head was spinning. She wished they could get off the damn boat and talk on solid ground.

"Last night over paella."

"You had 'so-called paella' at my parents' house?"

"Why 'so-called' paella?" he asked. "It's delicious."

"What were you doing there?" she demanded.

"Your mother said I had to ask your dad for your hand in marriage," Jon explained. "Even though we both know she runs the show."

"You asked my dad for my hand?" Sofia was screeching now at an unattractively high pitch. "And you kept all this from me?"

"I don't know the rules," he said. "It's not like I do this every day. Was I supposed to ask your permission to ask your dad? Is that how it works?"

She waved her hands before her eyes. Another pressing question came up. "Were they nice to you?"

Her parents must have been stunned. They'd only met Jon for the first time on Father's Day. At the restaurant, before he'd arrived, they questioned the wisdom of inviting a "newcomer" to the most sacred of family events. Her mother noted that Miguel hadn't invited any of his interim girlfriends to dinner. That had pushed Sofia onto her feet. "Jon isn't an interim anything," she'd said. "You all better be nice!"

Eventually, they'd mellowed. Jon worked his magic and before the meal was over, he was making plans to catch a baseball game with her father and Miguel. Her mother, though, had been more reserved. It generally took her a long time to warm up to people. And now, to have this new man show up talking marriage, it must have thrown her for a loop.

"Your parents love me," Jon said.

She cupped his face and kissed the cocky expression away. "Tell me the truth. Did my mother put you up to this?"

Sofia wouldn't put it past her mother. That woman was obsessed with marrying her off—as if matrimony was the only path to salvation.

Jon put the ring back in the box. "You're impossible to propose to."

"I'm sorry. I don't know where all this is coming from."

"From my heart," he said pointedly. "I love you, Sofia. I want a life with you, and I want your family to be a part of that life."

Sofia fell quiet. She really was impossible. She'd questioned his motives, doubted his sincerity and come up with excuses to reject his proposal wholesale rather than consider it with an open heart.

"Let's start over," she said brightly. "Let me see the ring again."

He pocketed the box. "No."

She went to him, rubbed her cheek against his and purred, "Let me see it."

He took out the box and opened it, revealing its white lining. That ring! A square-cut canary diamond bracketed by two smaller white diamonds that drew out the fire in the yellow stone.

He loved her in color.

Sofia shut her eyes, fighting its power. "I can't look at it. Put it away."

"You're saying no."

His voice was flat with disappointment.

Sofia drew him onto the bench. She spoke as gently as she could. "I'm saying 'not now.'"

Jon snapped the box shut again, and Sofia grabbed it from him.

"You're not listening," she said.

"You've made your point."

Sofia changed tactics. It was time to speak to him in a language he'd understand. "Look," she said. "How about this? We'll put this ring somewhere safe. You keep the house. I'll lease an apartment for one year. When the lease is up, you propose again."

Jon, though, couldn't simply agree to her terms. He had a counterproposal. "One year lease. No renewals."

"That's fair."

"Let's say I agree to this," he said, "and in exactly one year's time, I propose to you again. What will be your answer?"

"Will one year be enough for you to work on your proposal?" she asked. "As it is, it's kind of rocky."

Jon looked away, shaking his head.

"The ring is phenomenal," Sofia added to soften the blow. "That's a start."

He faced her. To her surprise, his eyes were tender. She couldn't help but tear up when he sank to one knee before her and took her hand.

"Sofia, sweetheart, you're my sun. I had nothing before you. You've given me everything."

"Jon…"

"Now," he said. "In a year, when I ask you to marry me, what will you say?"

A flare cut an arc in the evening sky. It exploded into

shards of light that rained down over the horizon. *Fire-works*. Sofia looked up at the spectacle, then back at Jon. With quiet confidence, she said, "Yes."

Epilogue

Eight months later...

The bride didn't wear white. She wore a silk slip dress the color of pearls. Her hair was swept back with diamond combs. A pair of blue satin pumps completed her look. She walked alone down an aisle fashioned out of rose petals.

The groom, in classic black, forgot the vows he'd written and memorized. Instead, he vowed to give her the world if she'd be his forever. The newlyweds kissed well before the officiant invited them to.

Leila and Nick were married in their backyard. From her seat next to Jon in the front row, Sofia couldn't help but dream of her own wedding. She'd wear organza and a veil long enough to trail behind her. She'd carry a bouquet of circus roses and wild orchids. Her father would walk her down the aisle.

After the ceremony, they ducked into the kitchen while the bride and groom posed for photos. Sofia had hired the caterer and they were treated to shrimp cocktail.

"What's the plan for tonight?" Jon asked. "Your place or mine?"

"Mine," Sofia replied. "I'm going to need industrial strength makeup remover."

Jon grunted. She scoffed and fed him shrimp. "Don't be grumpy. You love my place. You said my bed has good lumbar support."

He chewed and nodded. "I do like lumbar support."

Sofia winked. "Who takes care of you, baby?"

"Here's an idea," Jon said. "Let's get away to get married."

"We'd agreed on a backyard wedding," Sofia said. "Like this one."

"Not sure I want a wedding like this one," he said. "We can top this one."

"Jon!" Sofia looked around to make sure no one had overheard them.

He freed a lock of her hair from her bun and twirled it around his finger. "We could leave everyone behind. Wouldn't that be less pressure for you?"

She'd complained that her mother was driving her crazy. Sofia wasn't even officially engaged and yet her mother was planning the wedding. The unofficial theme seemed to be "more is more." Every day, she filled her email inbox with photos found on Pinterest and *Modern Bride* blog posts. But today, Nick and Leila's simple exchange of vows had reminded Sofia what was at stake. Flowers, ribbons and table decor were all great; expressing love was what mattered.

"How about a destination wedding," Sofia proposed. Instead of leaving everyone behind, they could take everyone with them. "We could go up the coast. Or maybe head back to Key West."

She had a vision of a beach wedding followed by dinner and dancing. They could make a weekend of it.

Jon leaned close and kissed her cheek. The kiss was more sensual than any peck on the cheek had a right to be. "We can go wherever you like."

He was so handsome in his white dinner jacket. Sofia wondered if they'd be missed if they ducked into the guest bathroom.

"You two behaving?" Brie asked.

Taking a break from her maid-of-honor duties, she joined

them at the marble breakfast bar. She looked lovely and edgy in a lavender gown, her long braids loose on her back.

"Never," Jon answered.

Soon after, Minerva joined them and the conversation turned lively. The caterer tempted them with a bottle of Veuve Clicquot. "Care to get a head start on the champagne toast?"

"Isn't that bad luck?" Minerva asked.

"Not for us!" Brie answered, laughing.

"Hand it over," Jon said.

"No," Sofia said. "Tonight, I'll pour."

She was in the mood to celebrate. She cupped the large green bottle, cracked the foil and slowly released the cork. Without fail, it made that sound she liked.

Pop!

* * * * *

COMING SOON!

We really hope you enjoyed reading this book. If you're looking for more romance, be sure to head to the shops when new books are available on

Thursday
23rd August

To see which titles are coming soon, please visit
millsandboon.co.uk

MILLS & BOON

MILLS & BOON

Coming next month

THE MILLION POUND MARRIAGE DEAL
Michelle Douglas

Sophie had had good sex before, but what she shared with Will wasn't just good. It was *spectacular*. She hadn't known it could be like this.

Not that she said that to Will, of course. It smacked too much of a neediness that would send him running for the hills. She didn't want him running for the hills. Not yet.

Not that they spent all their time in bed. They spent hours riding Magnus and Annabelle as he showed her all the places he'd loved when he was young. They explored the glens and the hills, traversed lochs and cantered through crystal-clear streams. They spent hours playing board games and watching musicals with Carol Ann.

But when they retired to their room each night — they made love as if they never wanted to stop. Not just once, but again and again. As if they couldn't get enough of each other. As if they were addicted.

It wasn't until Thursday, though, that Sophie finally realised how much trouble she was in. When Will told her he had to go back to London the next day. The depth of the protest that rose through her had her clutching the wedding folder she held to her chest. As casually as she could, she leant a shoulder against the bedroom doorframe to counter the sensation of falling, of dizziness. Loss, anguish and despair all pounded through her.

Will sat on the side of the bed, his back to her, pulling on his shoes, so she allowed herself precisely three seconds to close her eyes and drag in a breath, to pull herself together. 'No rest for the wicked?' she forced herself to ask, with award-winning composure.

He didn't move and she tried to paste what she hoped was a cheeky grin into place. 'I suppose I should be focusing on the wedding anyway. Nine days, Will. The month has flown!'

He turned, a frown in his eyes. 'Do you want to back out?'

'Of course not.' It was just… She hadn't known when she'd agreed to this paper marriage that she'd be marrying the man she *loved*. 'Do you?'

Continue reading
THE MILLION POUND MARRIAGE DEAL
Michelle Douglas

Available next month
www.millsandboon.co.uk

LET'S TALK

Romance

For exclusive extracts, competitions
and special offers, find us online:

f facebook.com/millsandboon

⊙ @millsandboonuk

🐦 @millsandboon

Or get in touch on 0844 844 1351*

For all the latest titles coming soon, visit
millsandboon.co.uk/nextmonth